The Story That Had No Beginning

The Story That Had No Beginning

Daniel Kemp

Copyright (C) 2018 Daniel Kemp
Layout design and Copyright (C) 2021 by Next Chapter
Published 2021 by Next Chapter
Cover art by Cover Mint
Back cover texture by David M. Schrader, used under license from Shutterstock.com
Mass Market Paperback Edition
This book is a work of fiction. Names, characters, places, and incidents are the product of the author's imagination or are used fictitiously. Any resemblance to actual events, locales, or persons, living or dead, is purely coincidental.
All rights reserved. No part of this book may be reproduced or transmitted in any form or by any means, electronic or mechanical, including photocopying, recording, or by any information storage and retrieval system, without the author's permission.

Other Work By This Author

The Desolate Garden
Percy Crow
What Happened In Vienna, Jack?
Once I Was A Soldier
Why?

Novella:
A Shudder From Heaven

Children's Tales:
Teddy And Tilly's Travel series
The Man Who Makes The Clouds
The Mermaid Who Makes The Seas
The Mother And Son Who Make The Fun

For a lie to add piquancy to a story, the story would be factual. Fantasy needs no lie to stimulate or excite. But if the factual story is contrived or fallacious then it's the fantasy that is the truth.

Part One

This story has no single definitive point in time when it could be said to have started here. It cannot be said that when Alice and I were taken into two separate foster homes at the age of eight our lives would cross the paths of the three others in this room but we would never meet again. Life is capricious enough without wild assumptions having a say in the making or the delusion of providence holding the deciding ace in any predetermination.

If I were to list the catalogue of misdemeanours I committed as a juvenile, or the petty crimes I was involved in as a young man, then add the violence of my later years, none would fully explain what led my twin sister to ask the opening question of her three invited guests this night, nor would one find any connecting items of merit in the achievements of the participants in the conversation. All of those antecedents help to paint the background to this tale, but the finer strokes of the artist, those intricacies of details from shade to light, are yet to be found in the shadowy past of us five. Yes, we are five; four to dinner and I make the fifth guest. I was christened Tom Collins and occasionally I live in this house. My relationship to these four is crucial; for now I'm dead.

My sister differed from her night's companions in many ways but, not it must be said, in the financial standing that a passer-by might use to measure another's success. She was not born in the same social bracket that the others come from. No birth endowments had been bestowed on her. She deserved her membership to this club by right. She had earned her place. Now, however, she had reason to regret working her way up the same social ladder as those sitting around the yellow linen covered table, adorned with sparkling silver cutlery, empty white china plates and cut glass. Her style complemented the symmetry of her surroundings dressed in a pale, blue chiffon low-cut dress bought especially for the occasion from a designer boutique she favoured in Chelsea Green, just behind the King's Road. Her vocation of photography had paid well, allowing the cultured surroundings that she had always longed-for, far away from the sins of my own shabby life.

* * *

"Do you think lying is endemic in society today? I ask because earlier I was in Harrods when I overheard a woman telling her son of about six or seven years of age that all the oranges came from Spain where apparently her family had a home, surrounded by orange trees. At first, I presumed she was trying to instil a sense of importance in the boy's mind for that home in Spain, but then I thought no, a lie is a lie. I confronted the woman and she confirmed my first impression. She was indeed commending Spain to the boy's mind and nothing more. She was very upset when I said that it was a lie she had told her son. She couldn't see it as being important. What do you think, Giles? You deal in lies almost every day of your life."

Sir Giles Milton was one of only a handful of QCs, Queen Counsels, to be appointed before completing the usual fifteen years of practice as a barrister. Scotland had been his birthplace, but you would never know that by his accent. He was the fashionable face of an advocate: six foot four inches tall, black-haired, olive-skinned, narrow hazel coloured eyes with a handsome charismatic face that had adorned the covers of four top-flight magazines for his defence of a multimillionaire accused of murdering his equally rich new wife whilst honeymooning in the Seychelles two years and some months prior to tonight's meal. Giles was educated at Christ Church, Oxford, where the Christ Church manner of assumed effortless superiority is born. He believed that the world should primarily be regulated for the benefit of those who were at Christ Church. He waded in popularity as would a hippo. Low flying blandishments and strangulation by his own honeyed words were the only dangers he faced. At the age of forty-one he considered he had conquered the material side of his world. Tangible wealth was not his God, but prestige and veneration were.

"You're not correct in the terminology you used, Alicia. It is not lies that I present in court. If everyone who appeared at the bar dealt only in honesty, then there would be no need of me or any well-remunerated barrister. There are mitigations to truth, or, as some people see it, a different story to tell. I am just the simple vessel through which those account flows. The example you give is innocent enough and I'm sure not meant to deceive the young boy into believing that all the oranges grown came from Spain. If that was the intention then ultimately it would fail as the boy would either view displays from elsewhere or become aware of imports from countries other than Spain as he grew. Although, technically you are correct inasmuch as it was a lie, it is a lie of no consequence. It was not said to permanently hoodwink the child, but simply as an extravagant stretch of the truth in order to magnify the significance of the family's home in a foreign land and thereby cross invisible boundaries that may exist in the child's mind. It could also be a challenge for the boy. One where he exercises his imagination and extends his education."

"Is that what a jury does when listening to your trial summery, Giles; use their imagination on your verbosity?"

That question was asked by Susan Rawlinson, formerly Barrett, editor of a national broadsheet newspaper and at thirty-eight years of age seemingly assured of a bright, rewarding future. Susan was an untamed beautiful, blonde haired, self-assured woman, capable, intelligent and determined, having succeeded in the majority of her ambitions. Her God was not wealth either. Hers was one of further recognition within the pitiless world of journalism and the literary acceptance of her soon to be published second novel on which my sister's photograph of her enriched the front cover.

"Isn't it quintessential imagination that spurs you on, Susan? A little leaning to one way or the other when it comes to reporting the news to stimulate the average reader who has no real interest if it's not about immigration or sex?" Giles retorted.

"Bloody hard to find anything sexy in the rag that Susan's in charge of. All anti-Tory bullshit if you ask me."

And there we have our third and final guest: Rupert Barrett, called The Bear after the comic strip character much loved by his late mother. Chiselled, square jaw with a feral, craggy face. A winter man; bleak on the eye and raw to the senses. Once a revered English rugby union star and now the owner of 'Bear Cave,' nightclubs, places catering for a wide variety of night-time tastes, predominately in the north-west of England. A sturdily built man with brown hair and hazel eyed and the same lack of personality as any one of the many men he employed on the doors of his five nightclubs. His goals in life had all been fulfilled; adulation, fame and wealth, but those without personalities have few wishes beyond the materialistic and Rupert was no different in that regard. Susan and Rupert had been seeing each other, occasionally living together, over a shorter period than a year. It was a turbulent relationship no more so than when Rupert criticised Susan's left-wing ideals.

"When was the last time you read anything other than a comic book or bothered to watch anything other than the sports news, you big thick bear?" The question was asked with a smile on Susan's face but a dagger hidden in her voice ready to stab him if the answer was not to her liking.

"What's the point? All news reporting is as I said, biased in one direction or the other." She indulged him, but Alice did not.

"Do you not believe anything that's reported in newspapers or on the news, Rupert?"

"I stopped believing newspapers when I met Susan, Alicia. She's too beautiful to be bothered by the truth. As for the news channels, I think they're sponsored by their individual political lapdogs with the idea of making ordinary people feel guilty if they're not giving to one or another charity to save the world. Do any of them report good news? No, not a single one! But good things do happen. There're not reported because people might start thinking, hey ho, this life ain't so bad after all. Let's start living it up a bit without the guilt of the whole of Africa sitting on our shoulders. Let's go clubbing and dance the night away thereby putting more money in my tills." His laugh split the room with a *ratatatat*, like a machine gun opening up in the stillness and silence of a high vaulted church. Giles smiled smugly, sharing Rupert's knowledge of how beautiful Susan was. Susan smiled stoically, well versed in Rupert's views on charity and governments, whilst Alice forged onwards.

"So you agree with me about lies being the currency of today's world, Rupert?"

"Yes, I do. With news reporting it's because the journalists either want to be, or are told to be, newsmakers. I know I'm seldom told the whole truth by the managers in my clubs. That's why I employ a couple of real heavies to make sure the pilfering doesn't exceed what I budget for."

"Are you saying you threaten these managers of yours, Rupert?" Giles asked, feigning surprise with widened eyes.

"If you know a better way to stop someone else's hands in what's mine then I'd listen, but surely, Giles, isn't what I do the same as the punitive justice system you represent; hold a rod of iron over would-be wrongdoers? That's if they're caught of course."

"Do you punish those managers who do steal from you, Rupert?" Alice asked naively, but it was Susan who answered.

"Where are you going with this, Alicia? Of course he punishes them. What business owner wouldn't? Would you want him, and all those involved in commerce, to include wording in the employment contract to reflect the degree of penalty imposed in proportion to any theft? Steal a bottle of water and your contract is torn up. You are flogged for the theft of a sandwich and if you dare to pocket an apple without paying then kiss your life away as the executioner sings *God Save the Queen*, swinging the axe." Her sonorous voice resonated around the room.

Giles beckoned the man dressed in white livery who stood by the window overlooking the Thames, to serve more of the opened champagne that rested beside the other bottles on the antique serving cabinet. Skilfully he glided along both sides of the oblong dining table refilling the crystal glasses then returned to his position and effortlessly uncorked another Dom Pérignon, placing it back in its bucket of ice. Impassively he gazed across the river, noticing the floodlights now ablaze in Battersea Park lighting the football pitches, oblivious to the conversation in the room having 'waited' at several dinner parties held in the more intimate surroundings of a home instead of the restaurant where he, his wife and the chef once plied their trade. He did not know it was near those lights that I had died. That night, the night of my death, there was no reason for the lights to be on. However, if speculation is a game you enjoy, then the question of whether or not the lights being switched on making a difference, is, I expect, one you would like to be answered. As it was only I and one other hiding in the moon cast shadows I feel qualified to end your speculation. My answer would be an emphatic no, as I believe I was destined to die in the way it happened.

* * *

"I imagine it's already there to some degree - thou shall not steal from thy employer - or words to that effect," Alice replied as her glass was replenished. "After all, domination is the only philosophy that's lasted since the beginning of time. But that's not my point. I wondered about the lack of honesty that is undeterred by any amount of threats, be they administered in Rupert's way or by the threat of prosecution in a court of law. Where once was intuitive integrity there now seems none and I think all three of your professions embrace and perpetuate it." She sipped her champagne and waited for their response. Now it is you, the reader who must wait. Longer than my twin and for a different reason. Nonetheless, wait you must as I reminisce of what's gone by and tell more of my sister, Alice.

Here in my own special purgatory, where I expect my sins are being counted and then used to determine my eternity, I am at a loss to know why this power to see Alice's past has been granted, nor why I can read the minds of those around her who have influenced the paramount phases in her life. It would appear that my vocabulary has grown beyond all recognition to those I used to be associated with who, if listening, would never know it is me who speaks. I suspect the dinner is where my knowledge will end, along with my newfound eloquence, as it's the past and not the future I am cursed with. I have no idea how this night will unfold for the four who participate at the dinner party. All I can do is recount the story as it is shown to me without any interpretation, but bear this in mind as you continue to read. As I have been granted this ability to see the mistakes made in lives other than my own, are similar people such as I reading your thoughts and your hidden secrets as you indulge yourself with me? If so, then the skeletons in your past are being interrogated as I hold your attention.

Part Two

My sister and I were born within an hour of each other at number 5 Alice Street, Bermondsey, London; at the Bricklayers' Arms end of Tower Bridge Road.

Collins was our surname, but my sister was not baptised Alicia. No, that name would not have existed in our parents' unimaginative survival. She was named Alice after the street, and I was originally named Tom as our mother, Rose, had a very bad period of pregnancy. Tom and Dick being London slang for sick!

Charlie, our father, was at the time of our birth a railway worker. Plying his trade in the sidings of both nearby London Bridge and the goods yard at the Brick, both within a quarter of a mile of our three-bedroomed terraced house backing onto the jam factory. He was, as I understand, an engineer of sorts, but what kind I was never told. Unfortunately he was not around long enough to bridge that gap in my education, nor was I interested enough to ask. I should now be at that stage where more information would be something that I hunger for, just in case we bump into one another and I can say, "Hi, Dad! How did you make so and so in your day?" Bluntly, I must tell you that I didn't give a toss then, and I don't now.

He died when we had lived barely eight years of life leaving me with few recollections of him other than of a tall but seemingly always stooped man, solidly built with a wheezing cough, who whenever I saw him was sitting in the same chair against the same window in the local pub. He never seemed to look away from that window and never gave either of us a smile to lighten the days we spent suffocating in the putrid air from which there seemed no escape. If I did see him at home, I cannot recall when. There are other small snippets that I can summon up; one being his death, but that I will tell of as this story unfolds. The same year as losing one parent we lost the other. Our mother died from a combination of lung cancer and misery, and again I must confess my ineptitude in not knowing what caused her the most pain. I had not helped the situation but only now, in this state of retrospection, is it possible for me to recognise this element of self-absorption that had obviously started early and never changed. If you are beginning to believe that you'd be wise to have a handkerchief close to at hand to wipe away the tears this story could evoke, then I must disappoint you, as any sympathy for my demise would be wasted along with your sorrow for the way I lived my life. When I did draw breath I felt no emotion of warm-heartedness towards anyone. In this, as in many things, Alice and I were mismatched. She had an altruistic side that I would never have understood had we stayed close.

Approaching nine years on from our separation I was an imposing figure, one of six foot three inches tall, wide at the shoulder and narrow at the waist. I weighed over fifteen stone without an ounce of excess flesh. My big hardened hands were used to being bruised and bleeding from contests of a pugilist nature in its rawest state of bare knuckle fighting and my face carried many marks to authenticate that participation. I had a scar above and below my left eye that had been caused by a ring worn by a travelling boy when he was nearer twenty than I was to fourteen. That ring now counted amongst the three that I wore, all won in fights against older opponents. My nose had been flattened several times and was beyond salvation. It was the feature that most epitomised me yet not the one I prized the most; that was the photograph of a hooded me with a sawn-off shotgun in my hand robbing the post office in Newington Butts that was plastered on police bulletin boards across London, despite the publicity I was never arrested. It was one year after that robbery that I became aware, and in need of, a safe deposit box. It was after I had opened one in the City of London, not far from Liverpool Street Station, that I saw Alice for the first time since being parted.

I had seen an advertisement of a company who specialised in such amenities and made my way there. I entered London Wall House and took the lift to the basement then followed the arrows to The Metropolitan Safe Deposit Company Ltd. On pressing a button, beside a formidable steel door fabricated to resemble a wooden one, a light appeared in the blacked out window alongside it followed by the silhouetted outline of a face and a monosyllabic voice, distorted by a microphone, asked the forthright question.

"Yes?"

"I want to open a box," equally succinctly I replied. The voice spoke again.

"Push the door hard," it stated as a buzzer sounded and a flash from a camera behind the glass suggested I had been photographed.

A short unlit corridor lead to an anteroom room sparsely furnished with two matching soft, floral upholstered chairs with a low square table in-between on which sat a vase of fresh assorted flowers, next to a neat pile of out-date magazines. There were two black painted doors set in the opposite wall, one of which had a small reinforced, square glass window. Above the doors were two cameras. Framed landscape prints were on three of the walls, and a list of terms and conditions on the other. The carpet was workaday and unimaginative as was the overall colour, a shade of beige that the overhead hidden uplighters turned white where they shone. It was a sterile waiting room where the almost silent air-conditioning was the only noise. A few minutes passed before the windowed door opened and I was joined by a middle-aged man elegantly attired in a blue suit with a white shirt and yellow tie. I was slumped in one of the chairs.

"Good morning, young man, you would like to open an account with us, I understand?"

"A box actually!" I stated emphatically without moving.

"Yes, it is the same thing, only we refer to it as an account because there is an annual fee payable and various forms to fill out. I must say you look a little young for the services that we provide, but the world marches to a faster pace than I am accustomed to nowadays. Would you mind if I were to ask your age?"

"Yes, I would. I haven't come all this way to give you a list of my life's yearly achievements, nor to answer your next original question about why I'm not in school. As I say, I only want a box. Here, take a look. I'm old enough to pay rent." I handed him my fake rent book.

"We have a minimum age requirement, that's the only reason I ask," he replied apologetically as he looked at the document.

"What age might that be then?" I asked.

"Eighteen," he said, raising his eyebrows in an inquisitive manner.

"That's lucky! I was eighteen three days ago on Monday." I responded contemptuously.

I followed him through to another room, this time with all four walls lined by various sized locked drawers or cabinets that served as 'boxes'. There was a private, windowless 'room' in the middle of the floor, with a table and a single chair.

"Here we are, Mr Jennings, this is your box, number 2155. Don't forget the number please. Here is your keycard. Your photograph is embedded in it and you will be asked to swipe it through an electronic reader each time you visit. The reader is beside our front door. We don't have keys. As you can see the card has nothing on it to indicate where it's from or what purpose it serves; nevertheless, it does represent a security risk if it's lost. Keep it safe. There is an appreciable charge if you lose it."

I used the 'room' to empty my money, carried in a plastic shopping bag, into my allocated 'tray' then slid it back in the wall. It locked closed automatically. I caught the lift back to the ground floor level, and the street outside. I had filled in the forms with the false name of Terry Jennings and the address of an old man living in the block of flats on the Aylesbury Estate, at the Elephant and Castle. It was there, with his forced agreement, that I was going to make my permanent residence, which I did later that day, but not before I saw my sister.

* * *

Do you study people as I used to? Ever noticed how most walk the pavements too preoccupied in their own world to notice what goes on or who passes them? That's how pickpockets blossom and contrive the art form of invisibility. I was too big with cumbersome hands for such a vocation but I enjoyed the fanciful speculation of its employment on unsuspecting passers-by as they traversed the ground with eyes glued to it, perhaps consumed by thoughts of mythical gold or simply averting their gaze whilst searching for a form of privacy in such public places. For others it is their usual mode of life, uninterested and unconcerned with things around them. Not like me in the slightest, and not like me that day after finding a new home to deposit my ill-gotten money. My style of walking was different from all the above. I walked with arrogance inside me, a pride and a pleasure in what I had become. My fixed stare carried the threat of violence that most avoided through choice, and those that did not would not do it again.

I strutted my way through the densely crowded walkways back towards Liverpool Street with the heightened sense of importance that the safely stashed away sum of eleven thousand pounds, plus change, gives you. That plain, unexceptional white plastic card had changed my whole perception of life. I was certainly not looking for trouble, nor looking for a long-departed Alice, who had for the most part entirely slipped from my mind, but I found both.

I saw her near the corner of Bishopsgate, about a hundred yards ahead of me and him shortly after. In our years of separation she had grown upwards significantly, gaining at least six inches to her once small stature. Where there had been no curvatures, there was now a woman's body still waiting no doubt to be completed, but nevertheless recognisable and obviously noticeable by the glances she was attracting from men and women alike. The colour of her long curled auburn hair had not changed and that was what gave her away immediately. She was waiting at the kerbside for a delivery van to clear a service entrance.

I shouted her name across the heads of those walking between us. "Alice. Alice Collins," I added when my first cry had apparently not reached her, but no acknowledgement came my way. I started into a jog, pushing through the intervening gaggle, when one individual objected to my haste and awkwardness.

"What the fuck?" he said as I barged through his not inconsiderable bulk. I was intent on ignoring him and the others who had turned and looked in his and my direction, but his size had slowed me, allowing time for him to grab my arm. He never gave me a chance to walk away and I could never resist a challenge.

His swearing did not stop, it escalated in volume and range of abuse, becoming fluid as his uncontrollable spittle splattered my face. My hesitancy in responding to his verbal attack only seemed to intensify his anger and rage, giving him increasing courage. Until at last, it manifested itself in a punch, which missed. He had started it, not me, but it was my blow that finished the proceedings. Unfortunately the fight was not over quickly and I was not able to chase after Alice, but I was able to leave the scene before the blaring sirens arrived.

Alice had not heard the commotion in the street behind, there were too many other things on her mind to have noticed it. One of the first things she wanted to do was to test her new identity in a new way. She ordered a Tia Maria and coke at the 'Railway Bar' next to the station. I can't be sure whether it was her appearance alone or the choice of drink that made the barman ask to see some verification of her age, but he did, and Alice as Alicia Collinson faced yet another examination of the falsified papers she carried.

"I've got a post office savings book with a date of birth, will that do, do you think?" It was here that a far more happier and untroubled period of her life was about to start.

"Let me pay for that," said a woman with a pronounced rhythmical dialect and a mane of lustrous black hair from the other end of the empty bar. In front of where she sat was an overflowing ashtray on an otherwise immaculately clean and well kept countertop.

The primary wave of impulse to hit Alice was full of refusal. The second, equally full and brimming, was to abandon the drink she had only heard of on daytime television being ordered by some starlet striving for sophistication in a badly budgeted soap opera, and run. Paradoxically, the third and final one had been diluted by the time it struck. It was to accept and see where it would lead. After all it was only a drink, she told herself, adding. What harm could that do? However, that pessimistic question regarding *harm* was misguided. The question should have been phrased - '*How much good could come from it?*' Alice's newly altered documents had passed the barman's evaluation and her supposedly preferred tipple stood neatly on its patterned doily before her.

You can call it what you like, be as sceptical as you like, show the same prejudice that affects every thought and action you take, but don't you inwardly crave for those days of innocence to return? Ones where having 'naive' directed at you was not an insult, or a bad reflection on your judgment, but the conceptual constituent of purity of a lost time when virtue was to be admired and morality not ridiculed by laughter.

Luckily for Alice she was still able to cling on to innocence, albeit by only her fingertips. The inviting offer behind the smile on this woman's heart-shaped face of a 'good lunch' was impossible to refuse, as was an answer to her first question.

"So, have you just arrived in London, or on your way out of it?"

"Neither! I was attending an art class around the corner from here and fancied a drink." My sister lied, as she was pavement painting for money.

"I would be of the same mind as the barman and book you down as too young for drinking. I'm Mary, by the way and I bet you guessed I'm originally from Ireland." She said as she proffered her hand as a greeting which Alice gently shook.

"You'd be right. I am too young. All the same, I'm also too impatient to wait for another year to pass. My name is Alicia Collinson," Alice's smile was full of the gullibility of the impressionable. Fortunately for her, Mary was not a persecutor of simplicity.

Mary O'Donnell was the antithesis of the hackneyed turn of phrase, men don't make passes at girls who wear glasses, as hers only added to the mystique she portrayed, drawing your stare to her face, mesmerised by what you saw. She and my sister had many similarities, both for a start were beautiful. Their hair colouring, although different, was striking and conspicuous. Both walked with panache and grace to the restaurant. Straight-backed, arms extended and dignified. Both sparkled with vivacity, animated in their conversation, as pasts were compared and the clichéd references to the summer weather made, or the suitability of various shades of cosmetics to contrasting skin and all the usual nattering that women at lunch find so fascinating.

There were palpable dissimilarities displayed prominently by their individual mode of dress. Where Alice's clothing was decided upon by lack of funding, Mary's stood out by the refined style of the most expensive fashion houses of Europe, and her selections from the menu were not governed by the price. My sister's first consideration was that; the pricing.

"I'm embarrassed by this place as I'm practically skint, Mary, and I can't accept your generosity whilst never being in a position to repay it. I suspect you'll say, never say never, but the truth is I have no job prospects and nowhere permanent to live. I go from squat to squat. I left school last year around the same time I left the foster home where I had been for nine years. I needed to stretch a bit more than I could there. This place looks expensive and it just wouldn't be right for me to stay and take your money. It was wrong of me to come. I thank you for the earlier drink and I apologise if you had other plans. I should have thought it through." She bent down to retrieve her satchel from where it rested against the leg of the table, and made ready to leave.

"I've got somewhere to be. It was good to meet you, and perhaps we'll bump into each other again. Thanks for the company and your understanding," she said, averting her eyes from her companion.

"Stay a second and hear me out, Alicia. Don't be so proud, we all have to start somewhere." Mary gently touched Alice's hand, making her brown, round eyes widen and the corners of her mouth curl upwards as she smiled maternally at my twin.

"Have you got any samples of your work in that satchel or is that as empty as your self-esteem? Look, I've virtually finished my work for the day, it's a holiday in America and the financial markets are closed there. That's what I do, work the financial markets, but I get bored when holidays happen. That's why the extended lunch-hour. It's not always this way." Still smiling she removed her hand and stared into Alice's eyes beseeching her to stay, and at the same time determined to keep the unhappiness she felt away from her face.

"There's a couple of things I've got to clear away back at the factory, that's what I call the place where I work, but it should take me less than an hour. I can leave everything else to my team. After lunch, why don't you come back with me to my cupboard of an office and have a look around, then we'll start the evening off by discussing your future? What do you say?"

"It sounds very good, but why an interest in me, Mary? After such hospitality it must sound rude to question your motives, but until now there's been nobody looking after my best interests, so why should you?" With a tilt of her head and a narrowing of her eyes, my sister asked.

"I'm not after your body, Alicia. I'm not a lesbian, nor am I into human trafficking if one of those ideas had crossed your mind. And by the look on your face I guess one must have."

"It had, but why, then? Why should you care what happens to me?" Alice's pleading voice demanded, desperately wanting to believe that there was more to life than what had already been thrown at her.

There was a weighty sigh from the otherwise convivial Mary as she parted with a grief that no other living person was aware of.

"What a salient question you ask first up, and how to answer it? Okay I'll try: When I was seventeen I had studied almost every aspect of the financial world that waited for me to conquer. Circumstances that would drive a market up and what drives it down again. How banks work on both the investment and equity side and what's safe and what's risky. What a hedge fund was, what was meant by derivatives. I had maybe three more years of intense study to become someone who was wanted in a world full of money, and men chasing it. I was so studious that my parents were worried I would need stronger glasses for the 'book eyes' they said I would get before I was much older. 'Go out for goodness sake,' they would say. 'Have fun with school chums for a change, even if it's for only one night'. I ignored all they said, until that one night came along.

"I was at the Boston Academy for Girls, in the States, and it was the night of the annual prom. My first chance to attend, what by all accounts was the highlight of the year. Mum and Dad made a big fuss about it all, having a special gown made for me. All lemon yellow with sashes and tassels. I haven't got any snaps of it, but it's so vivid in my mind that it could have been yesterday. My hair was backcombed and pointed over my ears and up more or less to my eyes. I wore the proverbial yellow ribbon in it, sounds corny now I know, but then, well, I felt just great, and on top of everything. I was looking forward to it like nothing else ever before. I was raped that night and got pregnant. I've never revisited the details of what occurred and I'm not going to now, but to my shame I got rid of the child. I had only one reason for that decision; I took away a life so that mine would be better than if I had kept it. At the time it seemed right. I'm not going to say I was forced into that decision because I wasn't. I did what I did based entirely on the happiness I thought I wanted.

"In any form of measurement that you trust, or any book that can be sworn on, whatever it was I was looking forward to back then, hasn't happened. I'm certainly rich and successful. I have each and every one of the trappings that go along to prove it, including the Aston Martin and a house here in the square mile. Being able to afford these clothes and to eat in nice restaurants is not happiness, Alicia, not real happiness. All of that must sound so feeble to someone who says they have nothing, and I don't want leave you with the impression that I'm some rich bitch who's just found morals. I'm trying to explain that I gave up more than a child when I had the abortion and I've never been able to find what it was. You, as an artist, might understand if I say the picture's lacking substance, there's no weight to it. Nothing to touch, and say here is my composition, the ingredients of what is important, not simply to look at me and count what I've got. That's for the ineffectual to count and weigh.

"There was a boy in Galway, in Ireland, that I thought I loved before I went to America. When I came back I thought he, Liam, would be the answer to make me whole. That wasn't to be. He had grown into a man and become the hallucination inside which I had tried to hide my shame. After I accepted the fact that he didn't want me, I worked hard on not repeating the mistake of falling in love with the wrong guy again. I've done very well at it, never meeting anyone I wanted to be with for more than a few nights. Both my parents died too many years ago to remember and, I'll be honest, I miss them. Yes, I'm lonely. I am like the house in which I live; full of emptiness. This is going to sound so wrong and perhaps even more selfish, but I don't want to be remembered as the woman who outran the men in that chase for money. I don't want to be judged only on what I've achieved in a material sense.

"Here comes my heart, Alicia. I hope you're good at catching. I've a crushing need to belong to someone, and for that someone to only want what's inside of me. I'm after the happiness that escaped at the abortion. It's simple really, I want someone to share my life with. That way I might get the chance to redeem my soul for what I've done. In exchange, they get my money opening the doors that would normally be shut in their face. I would ask nothing from that person, Alicia. No favours, no sacrifice, no compromise of sexuality, or ideals and certainly no pity. My ambition is to help that someone achieve all their dreams through their own endeavours and hard work but with me pushing the obstacles out of the way. If we can have fun, well, that's just fine." Mary's questioning eyes probed at Alice looking for the reaction she so desperately needed. Finally, she asked the unswerving question that exposed her fear of rejection.

"Do you want the ride that my lifestyle will give you, Alicia? Do you want to be what I need? Please say yes."

* * *

Mary wasn't revealing all the truth of the cataclysm in her life to Alice on that special day and it's impossible for me to say if she was ever going to. Be that as it may, facts are facts and her aborted pregnancy had left an irreversible certitude of far-reaching consequences. Mary was unable to conceive life ever again.

Part Three

Time flowed quickly and profitably in the busy life of my sister, echoed by the scratching and caresses made by her pencils and brushes in the attic studio, of the four-storey building that she now shared with Mary, who never broached the subject of giving birth nor the sex of the child she had lost when aged seventeen, eighteen years ago to the very day that she met my twin sister. That coincidence was not divulged either.

Number 54 Charterhouse Square London EC1 with its curved façade and in all its grandeur was now her home and workplace. Inside it was a lavish home from a different age, set in the middle of a fourteenth-century terrace of a dozen houses beyond a bricked gatehouse and which now saw spontaneity with more glamour added to its impressiveness. If there had been expense spared it was nowhere obvious. Alice slept in all of the bedrooms other than Mary's in the first week just for fun, then showered in all five adjoining bathrooms after her exertions in the well equipped basement gym. There were two libraries full of knowledge and wisdom not just packed with copies of economic theories along the lines of Adam Smith's *The Wealth of Nations*, nor full of arguments in opposition to his *free market* thesis. Autobiographies of powerful politicians stood side by side with novels by Brontë and Thackeray. There were poems by Houseman and Shelley slid in beside works of Pasternak and Dickens. An ecliptic array, but sadly not collected on cultural merit. The primary reason for so many was one of investment. Most were first editions or had been signed by an author or a notable friend in dedication. Other exquisitely furnished reception rooms were subjected to her full scrutiny and all passed with honours.

Each day for Alice was enjoyably packed to the hilt. She had enrolled at the St. Martins School of Art, a pleasant walk in the sun or a short bus ride away in the rain, for her first love of painting and continued her normal education privately, funded by Mary. She prospered in both, having her first exhibition in a chic Mayfair gallery just after her eighteenth birthday, and a few months later was awarded a 'diploma of notable worthiness' for the uninspiring academic studies she'd suffered at Mary's insistence.

Her benefactor kept every promise she had made the day of the meeting and discussed the future and the independent roles they would play in its outcome. One being the introduction to patrons who would propel Alice ever higher in her climb to success. EC1 became the hub of many, besides Mary and my sister. Caterers drove their vans across the uneven, aged cobble stones of the Square, fraught with worry of ruined hors d'oeuvres or shattered ice sculptures for the parties thrown at number 54, not as often as Alice would have liked, it must be said. She revelled in them and adored the company, never intimidated by conversations ranging from frivolous pop culture to classical art, or from the continuing war against terrorism to home-grown politics. The house was not only a place where Alice felt safe and wanted, it was where she found true excitement as well.

Mary spent lengthy hours in her chosen career, waking at dawn most mornings and returning late in the night, or choosing to working in her office at home, as stock markets around the world opened and closed. She moved from the UBS bank building, where she had invited Alice, back to the company she had been originally recruited from, Goldman Sachs in Fleet Street, for the increased recognition she was promised if her clients followed, and follow they did in droves. When weekends came, and time allowed, number 54 was festooned in fresh flowers and running alive with smartly dressed carriers of silver platters, serving drinks and nibbles. On other occasions, when more intimacy was required, the platters were exchanged for sumptuous filled tureens, and denims and skirts for black ties and evening dress for the formal dinner gatherings that were arranged in the Chippendale room. A pianist on the Bösendorfer tinkering gently in the background, more suitable than the flashing discos that reverberated almost as far as the nearby St Bartholomew's Hospital. Mary was liberal in her associations and personal behaviour, but always advised Alice not to become so.

"You never have to sleep with any of them to get what you want. You know that, don't you? Just smile at those who are pleasant and walk away from those that are not. Above all be true to yourself. Your talent will get you where you need to be. Never use your bedroom for anything other than sleep, and don't have casual sex for the sake of it." Mary was becoming the mother that my sister had never really known, and slowly Alice was becoming the daughter Mary had cried out for.

Never once did Alice awake to find a stranger emerging from Mary's room, never once was she embarrassed in such a way.

* * *

I was never embarrassed when I had the misfortune to find strangers at the entrance to my 'apartment' and neither were my neighbours who were used to such things happening outside my front door. I too was sharing, only my house companion was not as attractive as Mary. He went by the name of Wally, real name Albert Hammond, and our address was not as upmarket as Charterhouse Square; 62 Pritchard House, altered by some wit into Pilchard House. Another similarity I fortunately shared with both Mary and Alice, I never, normally, remained long in the company of my visitors. Mine were uninvited police officers, custody being a more operative word than company in my context.

I took over Wally's rent book when he passed naturally away in his sleep, a year after Alice's change of fortune. I paid for his quiet funeral and continued to pay the rent regularly. Nobody from the council bothered to knock to enquire into the old man's welfare and the neighbours believed I was a relative. I did not fill in any national census or local council papers. I was anonymous, except to the police who knew my name and what I got up to, ensuring they visited me regularly.

Again, mirroring Alice, I had widened my circle of friends, only in my case they were not friends in the accepted sense, more comparable to other thugs and gangsters with similar disregard for convention. Breaking into houses took on a new meaning to me. In an identical fashion to the majority of things in life it started rather small then grew in size, but I didn't wait for the time span of Darwin's theory to evolve. I charged into it, resembling the bull that was pushing Mary's stock market higher and higher. In the beginning, I chose conservatively, concentrating my many attacks on an area around Primrose Hill and its nearest environs. By the time I expanded my regions of interest, the simple method I employed had been honed to perfection. Smashing down the back doors of expensive houses , previously surveyed and suspected of bringing forth dividends, then a shotgun pushed into a startled face of whoever confronted me and the demand of 'give me all your money' screamed at the frightened stare, had never been performed which such panache. I deserved an Oscar!

My eagerness for more growth increased into mammoth proportions when on my seventh robbery I came across a horrified occupant of a lovely home, delving through the crammed contents of her open floor safe. I took the jewellery and money it contained, leaving without any alarming fuss. Despite that aura of self-restraint my head was buzzing with images of large safes with their doors flung open and part of Eldorado beckoning me from within.

* * *

The manager of the Barclays Bank in Highgate Road left by the rear car park entrance on his way home to St. John's Wood, and the four of us followed at a respectful distance. The plan had been worked on for about a week before this night in infinite detail, and now was the time to make it active. All four of us had guns and the resolve to use them if needed for escape. There was a wife and two young children to greet him as his key turned in the lock, and I ran down the path and pushed him violently through the opening. The other three quickly followed. The two children screamed and his wife froze, looking directly at me with her eyes wide in terror.

"We're taking your husband for a drive, so the faster he does what he's told the quicker he gets back to you lot," I turned from her and shouted into the manager's ashen face. "You're coming with me to open your safe." I was holding a gun to his head as his body shook with terror. George pointed his gun at the now subdued trio, ushering them to a sofa in the lounge. One of the children started to sob, quickly followed by the other, then the mother too. They were forcibly gagged and tied and soon they were a sodden clump of bodies writhing and thrashing against each other, seeking a solution to the dilemma that was nowhere to be found.

"If we're not back in half an hour my mate here will shoot the lot of 'em. You do understand that, Mr Manager? Say yes out loud if you do," I shouted at him through the gap in my black balaclava hood.

We threw the man into the car and laid him on the floor for that short journey back to his bank, and I could feel his fear through my feet that rested on his trembling body. George had remained at the family home and Paul stayed in the car as Eddie and I followed the terrified man into the back door of his bank. It went effortlessly and a little shy of two hundred thousand pounds went silently swimming into our greedy sweating palms held upwards in expectation of more. It wasn't to be that simple. Paul had removed his hood to smoke as he sat and waited in that deserted car park overlooked by a camera he had forgotten. His stupidity was not forgotten nor forgiven by me.

I had just about enough time to sample the asinine voices and sanitised air that my ever increasing deposit of monies could pay for, before the police were forcibly leading me away from my fourth-floor rented flat. At the trial, neither the banker nor his family could separate us. For health reasons, that I will allow you to guess at, Paul admitted that he'd organised it all to which the three of us woefully agreed, readily accepting the sentence of four years' imprisonment for participating, instead of the eight for its inception. I behaved impeccably when away, especially when informed of Paul's accident in another prison far away from my own. He had inexplicably fallen down four flight of stairs, breaking his back in doing so. I showed great consideration in asking permission of the governor if I could write to his family and contribute in some small way to the permanently needed wheelchair he had been confined to.

Prisons in many ways reflect the world at large; there is a structure of obedience and rules to obey. There are good prisoners and bad ones, some who can cope and others who can't and there are also people who shouldn't be there. The same could be said of criminals and perverts who enjoy the freedom of everyday life. The comparability of those who can cope, and those unable to do so, are obvious, and the only distinction between those already incarcerated and those who are not, is they have been caught for their crimes. I served the whole of my sentence because I never wanted to be supervised on the outside as I would have been, had I agreed to be paroled. When I was set free I wanted to be free, far removed from the controlling hands of probation officers and the threat of being returned to prison for a misdemeanour of small significance.

* * *

I discovered in life that it is useless to speculate on what might have been. To want something that has gone is a wasted sentiment, one where grudges wander and despair is only a partially filled glass away. I have, however, nothing else to do than wonder what might have been had I found my twin that day in Bishopsgate. Having said that, and although I was not poor, I could not have competed with Mary on a financial footing, nor, it must be said, with the amount of time she did manage to devote to my sister. More importantly than either of those was how she exhibited an extraordinary example of benevolence for Alice to follow, whereas all I could have shown my sister was how to fight. My empty-headed regret was overshadowed by the upbringing Alice was benefiting from.

The understanding of a situation after it has happened is not a clever thing, merely frustrating, particularly if it is you that the event has injured. Foolish or perhaps, if a more serious lack of judgement was involved, a charge of being injudicious or one of carelessness may be levelled. In my case none of those descriptive words apply. What does, however, is every superlative to describe ignorance and shiftlessness. Here in death I crave for the power to make the absurd and contradictory happen. What I decried in life, that mentality of 'what if' or 'if only,' I find myself praying for more than any amongst you in the living, yet knowing if I did have that power, it is too late to relieve the immense disenchantment that overwhelms my sister at this dinner party of hers.

Mary's money opened those doors she had highlighted, one being choice. Alice consigned her passion of painting to indulge in only for pleasure rather than gain. She chose her newly acquired second love — photography as her discipline of commercial art and it was during a moment of complete contentment that she met the man sitting opposite her that night in Cheyne Walk. It was through luck that it came about; however, luck can be fickle …… can it not?

Part Four

Allow me to introduce another point where this story may have the beginning that I'm searching for in order to explain not only my death but my sister's preoccupation with the truth; Susan Rawlinson's book of dreams. When not dealing with news items of international or, conversely, little importance, Susan had an inquisitive side dealing in cerebral concepts and dreams and how the two are related in everyday life.

'To conceive an idea is to think in abstraction taking us to an intangible world that has no physical existence. Concepts are not limited to what we know, nor should they be. They are a progress through what we are aware of into the world beyond our material knowledge leading into our dreams. For example, if I were to say to you the word 'yellow', how could you relate to that notional word? You can only see it. You cannot taste, feel or touch it, but you see a mental image of the sun or a banana. In order to take our mental images and turn them into reality, you must first be able to compare then reflect and finally to abstract the speculative from the actual. These logical operations are essential in generating any supposition. You see three trees and compare them. You notice what the differences are between them. They have a different trunk, branches and leaves, but then you reflect on what there is in common - the trunk, the branches and the leaves. You then must separate their shape, size and contrast to validate the meaning of the word - *tree* - from its conceptual interpretation.'

That was a passage taken from Susan's first published novel which was about a psychiatrist and the close relationship he had with a female patient. She had used her own first name with a variation from her surname of Rawlinson to Tarrant. The story told of the analysis of her dreams with the contemporary philosophy that the psychiatrist applied to them, turning the concepts into reality. Although the work was entirely fiction, it had received many commendations from influential psychiatrists and psychologists worldwide. Leading to the invitations to speak of her book, and that's how she met Phillip Barrett who had accompanied Mrs Barrett to the event.

Rupert's mother, Mrs Barrett, was a clinical psychologist who worked principally in the hospital environment, a calling she had performed for almost all the eighteen years of her marriage to Phillip. The ending of that marriage came about in a tragic manner.

She was returning from Crowthorne, where she had been staying for a three-week experiment of a neuroscience evaluation on a convicted murderer and rapist committed to Broadmoor Hospital, along the M3 motorway making her way home to Wimbledon, in south-west London. It was atrocious driving conditions that Friday night with minds on the weekend and shopping to get with dinners to cook, or kids' Saturday outings. Margret was no different in being distracted. The traffic was heavy, but due to the time of night and the weather, reassuringly slow. In spite of the weather, the traffic in the opposite direction was light and travelling quickly. She was in the offside lane a safe distance behind the car in front, thinking about the report she had to write and Rupert's recent inheritance of the Barrett family home in Cheshire, on the sudden death of his paternal grand-father. It wouldn't have mattered what she was thinking of as there was nothing she could have done.

Phillip Barrett was one of four other husbands that night at Chertsey General Hospital along with five wives and a number of mothers and fathers, all identical in grief amongst the melee. There were two, however, who stood apart from the rest, as if ostracised by the others or perhaps feeling the guilt of their son. They were the parents of the young lorry driver who had, through bad driving, lost control of his vehicle, flipping over the dividing barrier and killing eleven people and injuring many more travelling in the opposite direction to him. Susan drove to the hospital to comfort her lover of less than a year and it was in her bed that night that he slept after the two had sex.

Phillip was a long-established civil servant, working in the Home Office rubber-stamping the licences issued by local authorities for night clubs of repute and some of ill-repute. He was also the final arbitrator on what was a legal sex trade establishment and what was not. That part of his job he found both pleasurable and well rewarding, sampling his own delights in as many premises as physically possible.

* * *

My journey to those halcyon moments of heady pleasure was initiated by an inmate of a prison where I was held, so it could be said that the beginning of my end was started by the words of a dealer in drugs. He was, as common parlance would describe, a mule or camel. Put in a different way, his transportation of illegal drugs kept the balance of imports over exports tickety-boo, and the boys and girls on the street in fine fettle. It could also be said from other mouths than simply his own, that his form of enterprise allowed gainful employment for the many who peddled what he supplied. For those who partook of his produce it could equally be said, that it allowed them to deal with the 'ups' and 'downs' of their lives in a more stable fashion. In his line of work he had been successfully avoiding capture for many years as he boasted to me, until of course, the last time that comes to us all.

In the great scheme of things being caught once doesn't normally count for much, but in his case unluckily it did. Unfortunately for him the judge listened more intently to the customs officers' hearsay evidence and to the police reports of known associates, believing them more pertinent than the words that came from my fellow prisoner, giving him an all-expenses-paid holiday of eleven years' duration. Eleven years of hell for someone like him. He had served five of those years by the time I literarily tripped over his effeminate body on a gangway leading to my own cell. There were three inside that chamber of persecution from which he'd been ejected, with none appearing at all interested in the dishevelled, discarded heap. That lack of interest quickly changed on my entering their cell. I didn't know for sure what the tormented soul on the walkway had done. I just didn't approve of the way they looked at me.

I would hope that my act of humanitarianism could be taken into account by whoever is ultimately to judge me here in death, but I doubt that person will be so easily fooled. I had sinned in putting my needs above those of the needy. It wasn't through a motiveless sense of kindness I had befriended this weasel; it was for future gain.

* * *

On the day of my release from prison I applied for a job for which I had no knowledge of there being a vacancy. I had knocked on the door of more than just the vicious employer of a discarded weaselling mule and camel, he was the most unforgiving man in the known criminal world. Only at that time, it was of absolutely no importance to me as to whether he forgave anything or not, nor could I envisage a time when it might be. As I said, I was absorbed by me.

"I've heard you're a useful bastard to have around, Tom Collins, very useful, they say. What puzzles me enormously is, how do you see yourself being useful to a man like me? I'm in a different line of work to you. People give me their money with pleasure written all over their faces. I don't have to take it from them at the end of a shotgun. Tell me what exactly you propose bringing to my organisation and how that could be of benefit?"

He was a broad-shouldered, tall man in what must have been his late sixties, if all the escapades I'd heard of him had been done whilst wearing long trousers. There was a two-inch long gouged out scar just above his right eye, a half-inch deep, which meant that at least one of the tales about his life was true, the one that told how he was shot in the face and lived. I never enquired into the validity of what had passed down the grapevine as to the extent of the damage inflicted on the brainless individual who had attempted that assassination. Nor did I seek verification of the widely held assumption of another who had abused this man's honour having his reproductive organs ceremoniously removed, whilst still clinging on to hopes of redemption listening to the dulcet melody of *Jumping Jack Flash* playing in the background. In particular the chorus line of 'Gas, Gas, Gas' to which the words 'Slash, Slash, Slash,' were reputedly inserted. The story went on to suggest that the shrivelled remains were conspicuously displayed whenever circumspection, or the requirement of less unreliable personnel, was being discussed. I confined myself to a silent state of examination whilst waiting for him to speak again.

His hair was thick and deathly white, swept away from his corrugated brow. Round faced with hollow cheeks of unblemished skin. A tailored white moustache curved around thin lips pointing towards a broad, undamaged nose. He had a square chin which emphasised a sturdy jaw line. His angry grey, sunken eyes drilled holes into me as if looking for a weakness he could exploit just as a prizefighter would stare before the confrontation. The contrasting portrayal of a businessman in his immaculate Armani black suit was deliberate and an intentional deflection away from the violent baggage of his past. I sat in front of a legend, a man few had seen and around whom the myth that had inevitably grown was more likely smaller than the facts.

"I understand that you were helpful to a *person* of my acquaintance whilst you were banged-up inside, Tom." He paused and stroked that facial growth while deliberating how to refer to one whom most called 'Mouth' for individual reasons, adopting the ambiguous term '*person*' as his preference.

"That was kind of you, but I don't suppose he's the sort of *person* you would normally help. So why was that? Why the change of character, I have to ask? You do understand my caution, I hope." With a bow of his head he invited my reply. I watched as he lit a huge fat cigar, thinking that one day I would be standing where he was doing exactly the same thing.

"I always wanted to work with the best, Mr. Henry, and I have forgotten how many times I've heard it said that you are the best. I saw what I did as a way of being noticed by you and getting a foot in your door."

He didn't hurry in replying, he didn't look the hurrying kind. More the purposeful sort who take their time over everything.

"Oh yeah, you got noticed all right, some of those cretins inside that prison actually believed I'd sent that *person* to them as a gift. Word had got around as such. One of those three you knocked about honestly believed I had arranged the transfer of that *person* purely for him. You just can't credit some people with intelligence, can you? Why would I do that, do you think?" The angry eyes had narrowed into questioning ones, as his head swayed slightly left and right expressing his bewilderment.

"I've no idea, Mr Henry." That was the trouble, I had and I was starting to feel a bit uncomfortable.

Instinctively I crossed my legs. He noticed my movement.

"Of course you haven't, Tom, because you are simple-minded and don't look further than the end of your dick. But and it's a big but, Tom, you seem to have more luck than some of my other lot. Don't go patting yourself on the back though. Being luckier than what I have already is no great badge of merit. In spite of that, I don't yet know if you have brains as well as luck. Did you ever stop to think that a man as powerful as I am might do something to stop animals abusing a *person* who worked for him? Maybe you imagined that I'm a heartless moron who allows abhorrent, disgusting things to happen to his nearest and dearest without showing disapproval?" He sat, shuffling his bulk into the soft upholstered chair behind his desk until he was comfortable, which I certainly was not.

"If I wanted him looked after I'd have done it myself, not got a buffoon like you to do it. He was a present to that one particular inmate, a personal friend of mine. I'd made a promise, Tom, and because of you I wasn't able to deliver on that promise. How do you think that makes me feel now?"

The door to the side of where he was suddenly opened and a man of colossal build walked in to stand behind where I sat.

"By the sound of things, pretty angry, Mr Henry. I'm starting to wish that I'd never come." I wasn't kidding. He leant forward and furiously glared at me. I instantly tensed and went to stand, but violence was not on order that day. With a nonchalant wave of Mr Henry's hand the man behind me moved over to the impressive array of bottles displayed in the opened drinks cabinet.

"Well, you shouldn't, it worked out well for me. Want a drink? By the look of you, you could do with one. You've gone a strange shade of pale, Tom, and you look at little bilious. Are you all right, or would you like to use the bathroom?" I managed a yes to the offer of the whisky and declined the bathroom.

"He felt instantly upset over the humiliation he had caused that *person* and thought you were one of mine. He imagined that I'd got the hump and turned my back on him, which would have meant his remaining time inside would not have passed in an agreeable fashion. Funny really, your antics made him think of other ways he could make me happy. Came up with some interesting offers very quickly, so everything's sweet and rosy. Never better in fact. Here, have one of these, and tell me what you're going to do for me." I uncrossed my legs and took his offered cigar along with the table lighter that masqueraded as a hinged tankard.

* * *

The general ambiance of Soho had changed over the years I'd known it from the outright seediness with girls in every doorway, or if not that, then handwritten signs advertising a *French Maid* or *Swedish Model* displayed above almost every doorbell, to the fashionable and popular eateries sprawling across pavements with roadside tables and chairs of today. No longer was it a place for the Francis Bacons or Oliver Reeds to spend days socialising over a few bottles of something, now it was the age of lattes with skinny milk and bottled water as the badge of the social elite. I'm not saying that everything of its past had disappeared, no, that would not be true as Mr Henry's *Kiss Club* stood witness to how not all change is desirable nor necessary.

The KC, as it was affectionately referred to by its clientele, was an impressive building in Dean Street with basement gambling tables, lounge bars and tailored bedrooms throughout its five storeys. The place catered for every desire. It was luxuriously decorated, comfortable and most importantly a discreet, secretive rendezvous for the upper echelons of the depraved and licentious with reputations that needed to be protected whilst enjoying their immoral pleasures. There was a vacancy, he told me, and I never enquired how it had arisen. I did what I was asked, keeping in the shadows, doing what Mr. Henry advised in getting to know 'who was who' before escorting some clients to restaurant tables or waiting wives in theatre seats after their participation in what the KC had provided for their earlier entertainment. It was not the drugs that Mouth had spoken about so often that interested me. The attraction for me rested with the prostitution and that was not in order to get something for free. Mr Henry's expansionist plans were along the same line as my own and, as he explained one morning before the club had opened, only now an option because of what I could provide him. However, you must wait again for that explanation as I tell more of my sister and her good fortune.

Part Five

Four years had passed in Alice and Mary's relationship when the bottom fell out of the European Debt and Futures market affecting thousands of those employed whose job was to manage such a crisis before it impinged on their clients and their holdings. Most were caught out, but the effect was not the same on the accounts that Mary handled; they saw a significant rise in the portfolios of their wealth. Her bonuses were huge and lavishly shared with Alice, who was still none the wiser as to the real reason for Mary's generosity. One thing Mary could not share with Alice was enough time, never having more than an occasional Saturday or Sunday to relax as the pressure of work increased in line with those bonuses. Business trips were the only holidays Mary took. To Alice, on the other hand, every day could be spent holidaying. Using Mary's brand new black sleek Maserati, she set out on a journey of exploration, but found what she searched for virtually on her doorstep.

From Brighton to Newquay, and almost the whole way back, the shutter of her camera had snapped at images that cried out to be framed, but none screamed out as loud as the desperate one outside the Wild Bean Café at the petrol station less than two miles from Charterhouse Square. That's where Alice found another beginning; sitting on the forecourt pavement begging for money. She could have used any one of several petrol stations on the way home but for some unknown reason, she passed them all in favour of this surreptitious one, on The Highway E1. It was meant to be. The woman's hunger-drawn, bony face with the harrowing tired and dirt-ingrained shadowiness of desperation gawked directly into my sister's eyes, pleading the question:

"Got any small change, luv?" she groaned as Alice passed on her way in to pay. The practised eye had noted the car, but the seasoned mind suspected that little would be coming her way from the driver. It wasn't cynicism or inverted snobbery on her part, just world-weary experience that told her so.

Those who've got it worship it too much to give it away. It's the working class that are the best at giving. They've had their shortcomings shoved up their arse so many times that they worry it could be them sitting here next.

The image this woman portrayed hurt Alice's senses, filling her with the visions she had attempted to push aside and never think of. Her mannerisms were not dissimilar to the numerous *street people* she had come across and her request showed no originality, nevertheless, there was a suffering behind those dirty green eyes that stared in a defiance that she had not seen before. The usual approach was one of deference; the more obsequious, the more guilt they imagined would be installed through self-condemnation. Never make eye contact seemed to be the standard, universal method of enticement to contribute. Here was the complete opposite, a look that demanded compliance. A look that dared even the most intrepid to pass without a glance at least. Behind that look was a captivating face that was impossible for Alice to ignore. The clothes were raggedy and filthy, nonetheless, the figure beneath was that of a young woman who in my sister's inventive imagination was more used to better refinements in aspects of life, than a cold stone floor on which to squat. The fascination was obvious and needed no one of letters detailing their expertise in one or other of the 'mental processes' to interpret it. Here was the contradiction to Alice's life had she not met Mary and here was the solidity of purpose and the substance of life that Mary had spoken of.

"I've got you a coffee and a sticky bun. My name is Alicia. I'm a photographer and I would like to take some photographs of you. I'm willing to pay for your time and I'm not asking for anything inappropriate."

"I'm not kinky or open for sex if that's what you're after. I may be desperate but not that much." Her look hardened, paying scant regard to the gifts as she greedily grabbed at them.

"Got rent to pay at the hostel, that's why I need the cash. Don't like coffee, but if you're in the mood to ease your conscience, a packet of fags with a cup of tea would help things along. They would disappear even faster with a nice crispy twenty-pound note in my hand," she added, opening the wrapped bun as compensation and in expectation of other gifts.

"No one can accuse you of being shy, can they? What brand of cigarettes do you normally smoke?" There was no smile of victory from the soiled beggars face, just a surly grimace.

"Any will do, can't afford to be fussy, can I? But I can be fussy over what I do for money, luv." Contempt tainted her reply mingled with recalcitrance but not inherent, one bred through necessity.

"How long have you been doing this?" Alice asked.

"Too long, luv. Too long to be suckered into something. Are you going to buy me those smokes? If not, I'd be obliged if you left me to get on with what I'm doing," she declared, spitting her hungry bites from the bun in all directions.

"Go and wait next to my car. I'm sure you noted which one it is. Don't touch anything whilst you're waiting for me."

Alice returned with two packets of cigarettes, placing a ten-pound note in between them and not the twenty she'd asked for.

"What's your name?" she asked as a car sounded its horn in frustration at being kept waiting so long. Her gifts converted the tramp's stubborn mood into one more amenable.

"Get in. We can talk elsewhere."

"Once I was called Georgia, but nowadays many names are shouted at me, some I couldn't repeat, not to someone with such a glamorous name as yours. The more respectable ones range from 'you crazy git' to 'spiky.' I think they mean my hair, but it could be my nature as I'm known to lose my temper now and again." Was there the slight semblance of a smile?

"Are you going to let me take your picture or not, Georgia?" Alice asked as she pulled away from the pumps.

"For another two packets of fags along with that twenty-pound note and the cup of tea you forgot, I will. If not, then no!"

My sister parked the car before exiting the garage and the few unprepared shots of Georgia inside and leaning on the Maserati, with the irony of hardship framed by a symbol of affluence did not escape the camera, nor senseless people in passing vans and lorries with their shouted obnoxious opinions.

"How did you get that bruise on your face, a fall or did someone hit you?" Alice asked, as the camera revolved in her hands skilfully snapping away.

"The apple must 'ave jumped out of the cider bottle when I wasn't looking, luv." She replied with the merest hint of a grin hiding her blackened teeth, but nothing could disguise her infused grimy hands with the torn, shredded nails.

The parody and the incongruousness of the scene was extended across the road in a small park with Georgia either kneeling beneath, or reclining and standing next to an old chestnut tree with its withered and vandalised branches. The significance of a proud yet unkempt, wretched homeless woman at no more than touching distance from a once wholesome healthy tree was astonishing in its simplicity. Around the corner from the Dock Street Hostel that was Georgia's lodgings, a café was found where a sign hung declaring: 'No Tramps OR Vagabonds Allowed.' Outside on the pavement and against the lamp post directly opposite the café door, more shots were taken using the backdrop of the sign as an emblem of defiance which was ingrained in those pain-torn eyes.

"Can I see your room in the hostel?" Alice asked.

"No, you effing can't, not without more money. Your twenty doesn't buy my life, luv! You've had your money's worth already. With a car like yours I reckon I've sold myself cheap." A commercial brain was emerging from beneath the surface of that photogenic face.

"I'll give you twenty pounds tomorrow for more shots inside, but I don't want you drunk. If that's what gets you through your day then leave it alone for once. I want you as you are now, no different and, with no one else."

"Make it a ton or there's no deal, luv. I want compensation if I'm not to drink tonight." Noisily she slurped her remaining tea, drawing deeply on a cigarette.

"'Ere, by the way, what happens if you sell those photos of me? Do I get more money, or do you pocket it all?"

"We'll have to see about that if it ever happens, won't we?" Alice answered.

"I want a deposit by the way. Make it a twenty," Georgia replied.

* * *

Mary made a phone call and within two months another gallery owning friend was hosting the provocatively named 'The Red Spiky George Exhibition' in his Cork Street, Piccadilly, art establishment with a list of sixty-four guests expected for the opening night. It was here that Alice met Susan with Phillip Barrett on her arm and a Marcus Allenby, who at one time had been Executive Director of European Equities at Goldman Sachs before setting up Allenby Venture Capital. Allenby had once been on intimate terms with Mary for an appreciable time. His was the first name on the short list, being an avid collector of photographic art.

* * *

"My interest is governed by profitability rather than artistic merit. I'm driven by the value attached to the name of the photographer or the subject. Preferably both if it is possible. I started my collection with some Eve Arnold originals of Marilyn Monroe along with some David Bailey's of Jean Shrimpton. I found them at the Portobello Market. You're probably too young to have heard of any of that. At the moment I have them on loan to the National Portrait Gallery, otherwise you could have come home with me to see them. I've got others though. The best ones hang on my bedroom walls. Same subject, very attractive women. They are my naked angels who watch over me when I sleep. If I could tempt you to come home with me, and then out of that divide dress you're wearing we could make comparisons. But no, not tonight of course, tonight we must concentrate on what is here. The ones you have in this exhibition are absolute stunners that even a philistine such as I can appreciate. You have captured the mood magnificently, I must say. Let me run your fan club and get you noticed, pump up your profile as it were. We could both make a killing. I have some ideas on that subject that we could discuss a little later in my Knightsbridge apartment. I have one idea you could be musing over until we can make an exit." Alice listened then smiled, making her excuses about mingling with others and made off towards the bar.

"If I were you, and I am only too aware that I'm not, I'd be very careful around that man. He's a bit of a lech." It was Susan who offered the advice.

"Oh, it's okay, I'm not that easy to impress. He wants me to visit some rugby club to take some pictures. Mentioned the showers as a good place to start before moving on to the bath. Said I would make quite a splash," Alice replied, still smiling at Marcus's suggestion.

"Did he! Sounds par for the course for him." Susan added with a sly grin. "I'm Susan Rawlinson and you are Alicia Collinson, the featured artist. Mary told me so much about you. It's such a shame she's in Switzerland. I'm positive she would have loved it and loved Marcus's humour. Has she seen the work you're showing?"

"Yes! She saw most before she left and I sent her some pictures just after I'd catalogued them all."

"The exhibition really is very good, a little too real perhaps for us sensitive types, but nevertheless brilliantly evocative. Reality can be so bitchy when it bites this hard, can't it? I've bought two for myself but don't tell anyone. Let it be our secret." She disclosed before taking Alice by the arm and leading her off to find Phillip in deep conversation with another guest.

The blue *sold* stickers appeared almost as quickly as the champagne disappeared, eventually covering every photograph of Spiky George that hung on the walls, keeping my sister fully occupied in a two-way flow of appreciation and gratitude of some soon to become owners of her work. Marcus Allenby bought several, and not only for investment purposes. He was one of the last to leave.

"Given any thought to my suggestion, Alicia?"

"Which one would that be, Marcus? Jumping into your bed or photographing naked rugby players? I've drunk too much champagne to remember how many suggestions you made."

* * *

In the life that I enjoyed until recently I came across Marcus Allenby when the tank was running dry for the acquisition of my sister's work, as the 'maybes, and we'll see' never materialised into anything other than fantasies, but the lust for a revisited fetish was once again beginning to gush. He was without friends the night I made his acquaintance but not without company. I supplied the two girls that made up his personal trinity in one of our very private rooms at the club. He was showing off, which was no surprise to those who knew him, to whom the habit had become natural and confused with largesse. He was that type of man who needed an audience to function. He carried the adulation he had enjoyed at Goldman Sachs into his everyday life, becoming his Valium and defining him for what he was. He loved being noticed, being the centre of the universe with his accumulated wealth buying his *friends*. The stock market had provided his excitement and buzz and the friendships that came fast and easy, but those that money can buy, can, with the lack of liquidity, slip away even more speedily. He was a long way from being poor, but his company had not survived the crash that Mary's clients had. The downturn in the near to home European economic climate had required sacrifices. No longer was there a yacht on which to entertain the impressionable hangers on, and only one property remained abroad for them to lounge in. His Christmas card list was shrinking, but his lack of depth still remained as large as ever.

Marcus was a greedy individual who wanted to eat from as many plates as he could, and to whom not only did art carry a price-tag but also the people he met. He was an enthusiastic collector of many things and an admirer of few. That lack of appreciation led to mistakes in his professional life, as well as his business one. He lost his Midas touch along with millions of pounds of investors' money. Alice was his last lover before a 'venture' he capitalised went disastrously wrong and he was confronted with two choices: adjust to the situation using what he had, or invent a distraction big enough to save himself from Mr Henry's wrath.

My employer, Harry to his close associates, had invested money in Allenby Venture Capital before the market nosedived into a vast abyss that Marcus had taken no precautions against. He was facing the prospect of losing a vast proportion of his fortune and his club. When Mr Henry heard that Marcus was in one of his rooms, he instructed me to fetch him and face up to his responsibilities. Neither man was in a good frame of mind when they met.

"I'm not talking peanuts, Allenby! I'm talking millions, pal, fucking millions! What you going to do about it?"

"Well, I was about to have fun with two of your girls before that moron over there dragged me away.

Now, I guess, I'll have to listen to you whining on about an investment gone bad. I don't make the markets, Harry. I just trade in them."

"Yeah! With my fucking money!"

"Yours and several others, including my own. Not all of you can shoot me and I'm not the type to shoot myself. Look, let's calm down. Nothing gets sorted out in a temper. Sorry, whoever you are." He was looking at me. "Never meant the label I called you."

"Pour *Nobbler* and me a Scotch, Bobby, then leave us to talk." Everyone had a pseudonym at the club, even the girls went by an assumed name. Bobby Brown was my name, both inside and outside the club. Marcus was *Nobbler*. I obeyed the instructions. I wasn't called back by Mr Henry, nor did I see him that night. I only became aware of the change the next day when I saw the name *Bear Cave* in neon lights where the *Kiss Club* was previously mounted. Mr Henry was pacing the empty ground floor corridor when I entered. His gaze travelled sharp end first at my heart when he saw me.

"You alright, Mr Henry? You look a bit edgy to me."

"Mostly because I've been waiting ages for you. Why don't you answer your phone? I have a job that needs seeing to, Bobby. One that requires your previous qualities of being an out-and-out arsehole." I silently followed him up to his office with mixed thoughts rolling around my head.

Part Six

The showing of 'Red Spiky George' brought more independence to go with the considerable fame now attributed to Alice. Number 54 became a location listed at every advertising agency in London, and Alice became the chosen photographer commissioned by them all. Everything from advertisements to film productions were shot there and if the house did not completely suit the product being advertised or the director of a film, then my sister was whisked away to the preferred location to weave her magic with her lens. Alicia Collinson was the byword used as the measurement of perfection and professionalism in the field of photography. The first and last definitive name on every advertising CEO's lips. It did not stop at that end of her camera. Manufacturers bid for her endorsement as did film processors. Her name alone became a commodity traded for money.

Alice was the wedding photographer at Marcus Allenby and Patsy Tomlinson's wedding and she didn't disappoint them or the multitude of guests. Marcus tried once more to feed the meter, whilst Patsy was temporarily secreted in one of the few lavatories of the wedding venue, crying as only the most redundant of us can do.

"You never did use the showers as I suggested, did you?" he asked, knowing full well the answer my sister would give to his question. Despite that, the suggestive twinkle still sparkled in his eye away from his bride of a few minutes. "Were you waiting for me to escort you there," he added.

When she stated that neither the showers nor him was ever needed, he pressed his desires further.

"I will always have an unquenchable desire for you, my dear, no matter how much my thirst has been satisfied elsewhere." He left the conversation with Alice's laugh of derision in his ears and she was left with a line to amuse any tedious dinner party of the future.

* * *

One morning a letter addressed to my sister arrived at 54 Charterhouse Square It was from:

Milton & Prentice
Attorneys at Law
6 South Square
Gray's Inn

London, WC1

Dear Miss Collinson,

The Law Society was approached by the University of California Press, an adventurous and innovative scholarly publication of America, expressing their desire to run an article comparing the differences between the legal profession of their country and the land where it all originated.

After considerable deliberation by members of the Society, Sir Giles Milton QC was chosen by his peers to be the face of English law and to appear on the cover of their magazine. He will telephone to arrange a visit.

Four days later the housekeeper answered his knock on the door at 54 and let him in.

"We fleetingly met at the Allenby's wedding, although, unfortunately we were not formally introduced and you were far too busy to notice or remember me. I'm Giles Milton and you are the famous Miss Alicia Collinson. I am here to submit to your every wish, Madam." With a narrow, tender smile he introduced himself, thereby resolving the omitted formalities.

Alice had noticed him at the wedding but showed no indication of having done so on the day; now, however, in the entrance hall she had no inclination of letting him know that.

"I understand you are to make me look so polished and sophisticated that our cousins in America will tear up their Constitution and add a back-dated signature to the Magna Carta. Do you think you can manage that?" he asked, adoring what again he cast his eyes upon.

It took two separate sittings for Giles's dignified face to become the acceptable front cover of the magazine, and two more for the inside photographs the American publication required. However, it took more than a mere four dinners at expensive restaurants for him to become acceptable to Alice. She liked what she saw, and liked him more as he slowly revealed the parts of a personality designed to ensnare my twin.

He had almost been married, so he told, a long time ago, when young and full of the aspirations of his breed. He had been accepted into chambers on the Royal Mile in Edinburgh, as a junior barrister with no office in which to hang his diplomas and certificates, but with a chance, as he described it to Catherine, the girl he so desperately wanted to make his own, to establish himself. She was as committed to the idea of marriage as he, but when she met the partners of the law practice a huge obstacle was placed in his way. She was, as the parlance of the day would have us say, of mixed race and defiantly not to their Calvinist liking.

'You must make your choice, young Milton. If you want to take up our offer then you cannot marry this girl.' He chose their offer, never looking back on that decision with any regret, but that was not the story he told my sister when on the verge of closing the gap to her heart.

"Catherine died giving birth, along with our son that she carried. I was heartbroken and could not look at another woman for years. I locked love away from my heart, Alicia. Will you help me find the key?"

By the night of the dinner party he had not changed his view on lies being justifiable; after all, he told them with as much confident ease as he listened to them.

"As a client you must never tell me the truth unless you want me to put that to the court. I cannot invent lies for you. I have a duty to deliver your account of what happened exactly as you tell it to me. However, I also have a duty to arrange the truth in such a way as to be to your advantage."

Blessed or cursed with this ability to see backwards into the lives of those close to my twin sister and in some cases, penetrate their minds, I cannot, nor would I wish to, understand the illogical reasoning behind a woman's doggedness in rejecting good sense when choosing a male companion. I had not thought of Alice as dull-witted, but helpless I stand in rationalising her choice. Perhaps my sister's judgement was blurred by his age, possibly he became an emotional substitute for our father, or maybe it was the trust she placed in his position in life, but something made her welcome his advances and the long journeys from the square mile, that is the City of London, to Cheyne Walk, Chelsea began. Could tonight be the end of those and the beginning of a new chapter of Alice's life?

* * *

Unfortunately Patsy Tomlinson's marriage to Marcus Allenby did not mean a new beginning for her. Patsy came from an extremely wealthy family where her only brother, older by almost sixteen years, Allan Tomlinson, was the Conservative Member of Parliament for Windsor-East and an occasional visitor to the Kiss Club. He had also invested in Allenby's company and, like Mr Henry, lost heavily. He had been introduced to Allenby by Phillip Barrett who, although not a paying member of the *KC* did on occasions take advantage of what Mr Henry offered as his inducement to smooth the passage of the licensing of his club. Barrett had a predilection for a certain kind of sex where two women would participate. One to tie him up and beat him whilst he watched the other woman having sex with a man. Tomlinson was always the 'other' man. I had heard rumours amongst the girls who performed this service that both men were gay and the addition of women to their shared sexual pleasure was simply a sham to hide Barrett's and Tomlinson's predisposition. Members paid for the room; who they invited and what they did in there was their business. If the girls who were requested into those rooms were happy to supply what was required then everyone was happy. Mr

Henry only had one rule: No violence towards the girls was ever permitted. This was my role within his empire, the one he had mentioned he never had the right man for until I arrived; the guardianship of the girls. I had the control that I wanted and the ears of all that I looked after.

Some of those that worked in the club were from Russia and the other former Eastern Bloc countries as the popular systematic circulation of hearsay would have you believe, but they also came from Torquay and Dundee, everywhere where dreams of money and fame can be found. The girls were the goddesses that most men, and some women, could only dream of, but others could afford to perform their fantasies with. They shared one important factor other than their physical beauty; they had enough intelligence to know how to look after the secrets they were told. I had different ethics regarding the retention of secrets and a different code when it came to sharing. They shared everything with me other than sex. That was a paying business, not a social exchange. It was the profit in their information, which was of incalculable value when passed on to the befitting people, that helped to enlarge the contents of my safe deposit box.

All the girls were housed together and had a strict working regime. No drugs, no excessive drinking, nor was a life outside of the Kiss allowed apart from with one another. They were a diligent bunch who worked hard and earned lots of money. The house in

Hertford Street, behind the Hilton Hotel in Mayfair, was where they found their home surrounded by the luxury they had dreamt of and where they could continue to daydream of their own 'Heathcliff' and the fantasy life of a kept mistress. The building, like quite a few in London, was owned by Mr Henry. I leased the property from him. You see, the Henry empire was built on people like me. We were the equivalent to subcontractors that he could legitimately say he knew nothing of. He just owned the buildings and let them out. He was a clever man who had clever advisors, one of whom was Giles Milton. Henry's office above the club in Dean Street had a different entrance than through the club itself; a flight of metal stairs from a covered alleyway and small yard at the rear in Richmond Buildings, a pedestrian passageway. Therefore a shake of the head and the 'I don't know what goes on downstairs,' was enough to legitimise his being there. He was never seen in the club when it was open and only rarely when it closed.

He owned other establishments similar to this one where he could have moved to and parked himself to count his fortune, but Dean Street had been the first of his empire and remained his favourite. We had spent long nights together in his office whilst he spoke about his business, and I lapped it up at his feet in the belief that one day it would be mine either by decree or by savagery. Until then I learned how to keep the girls happily engaged and Mr Henry's clients smiling as they paid their half-yearly subscriptions and fees for the entertainment they enjoyed. I was the pimp. I was paid from a bank account that carried no name I recognised. Henry paid rent for the premises in Dean Street to an off-shore company registered in the Maldives. I did the same for Hertford Street, except I deducted upkeep from the twenty-two girls who lived there. They were paid in the same manner as I, but they also kept hold of the considerable *tips* they were paid. The accountants helped us all to avoid paying too much tax and a happy prosperous life was had by all.

I had taken up permanent residence in Mayfair looking after my charges, relieved to be living beyond the fetid air of the Elephant and Castle or any of HM Prisons, but as Henry detailed the manner in which Marcus Allenby had manoeuvred the takeover of his business into Rupert Barrett's hands, I begin to feel the oppressive weight of degradation descending on me and I had no intention of returning to those previous squalid addresses. I looked for a way to avoid the obvious loss of life to come whilst we sat in his dimly lit office.

"How much of an arsehole have I got to be, Mr Henry?"

"I want that Marcus Allenby and Phillip Barrett to leak blood, Bobby. The two of them have screwed me."

"Do you want me to kill both Allenby and Barrett, boss?"

"Not today, Bobby, but one day I might. I want them sucked dry before it comes to that. I want that Allenby ruined and Barrett thrown on the scrapheap where he belongs."

I believed that my overheard secrets could be of use in the conundrum that I faced.

"I've heard rumours that Barrett has a male lover, a Member of Parliament no less. Could that be useful?"

"Who?"

"Allan Tomlinson! I took Barrett to meet him one day. I recognised him from the telly. He's always on it."

"Well, now aren't you the clever boy, Bobby." On the mention of Tomlinson's name a distracted Mr Henry leant back purposefully into his desk chair and gazed motionless at the ceiling.

"Hmm, that is interesting, Bobby. Is Tomlinson a member here?" he asked as he poured two glasses of Scotch and then offered me a cigar.

"No, boss, he ain't. I checked the register when the girls told me of him. *Builder,* Barrett that is, brings him every time he visits. They share a room and two of the girls, but Tomlinson never shags either of them. He likes being beaten as he watches *Builder* being shagged. But the girls say they're both gay."

"Allenby ever part of the company in any room they hire, Bobby?"

"Not as far as I know, boss."

"I need to damage Allenby's name somehow. Got any ideas on that score?" Mr Henry asked, reseated and staring at the ceiling once more.

"What's to stop us saying that it was Allenby who shared the room with Barrett? We can then get Tomlinson to say he was aware of it on the promise that we keep his name out of things, boss."

"A possibility," he said, lowering his gaze and sipping from his glass. "Could work," he added before dropping his guard and exposing a side I never would have known about.

"I had a fling with a Tomlinson back in the day. Fine looking woman, I seem to remember. Not a common name is it?" he laughed. That was the something I was unaware he was capable of doing.

He sat gesticulating as if he was a priest giving thanks to God by spreading his arms wide, waving his glass of whisky in the same hand as his smouldering cigar and his other as if he was the Queen, giving a royal wave. The scar on the back of his empty left hand, reaching from his index finger to beyond the shirt cuff with its sparkling sapphire cufflinks, kept capturing my gaze. It was an old scar which he had never spoken of, but it was the white outline, contrasted by his tanned skin, that caught the lights and kept grabbing my attention.

Everything about the man was manicured. From his fingernails which shone as he drew on that cigar, to his eyebrows which were bushy but immaculately trimmed. His thick white hair was smooth and glossy, swept backwards without a single strand out of place. His teeth were of a manufactured brilliance that whisky and smoking would have dulled if not. He placed his glass in the centre of the ink blotter on his desk and after carefully moving it until completely satisfied as to its exact middle position, he took a walnut from the cluster in an odd shaped glass dish and crushed it effortlessly in that gigantic hand of his, repeating, "it's not a common name," several times whilst resuming his merry puffing on his cigar. Abruptly he changed the subject.

"I wanted to spend more time with my grandchildren, Bobby. It's important to me to be a good influence in their upbringing. Point them in the right direction sort of thing. I've branched out over the last couple of years into more real estate, mainly abroad with commercial property home here, so I guess I should be pleased that Allenby's balls-up has forced me to sell to Barrett's son, but I'm not, Bobby. I'm bloody not! No one forces me to do a thing. You have your nose to the ground with those girls of yours. I want you to find something I can use against Allenby that will get in the newspapers and on the television. You will tell me if you hear or see something, Bob, won't you."

Two nights previously I had found something to use. The only trouble was I had gone outside Mr Henry's strict rules to get it.

Part Seven

I came across Susan Barrett by accident, not at the club but as a consequence of it. There was one girl amongst the many desirables in my stable that I took more of a shine to. Gabriella was Italian, having that appeal of being cool and distant, sophisticated and chic yet intimate when close and positively indecent when closer. Her demeanour and appearance with jet black hair and olive skin added to her stately aloofness, made her much more than simply attractive and much more than just sensuous. There was the extra tempting allurement of the natural seductress in her hot blood. Her dark green eyes were aware of what was wanted before having to be asked or pointed in the right direction. The soft awareness of her enchantment and magic held me, and many like me, spellbound and beguiled in a way no other could. She was the metaphoric jar of sweets just beyond your reach no matter how hard you tried to stretch that little bit more unless, of course, you could afford the artificial attentiveness she would supply. I could, if dependency on money was the only consideration, but had I paid her then I would have cheapen all that I worshipped most about her. As I said; she was the sweet beyond the grasp of my evil.

I have already declared that I never encouraged any kind of understanding with the girls employed at the Kiss. They weren't in the industry for fun and in any case women in general never found me to be attractive. The opportunity of being in a meaningful relationship with a woman did not occur, a regret of mine to put beside the rest. I would have liked it to have happened, but let's get back to the point, shall we.

Two night before the event that led to my meeting with Mr Henry, *Nobbler* had requested a home visit and asked for Gabriella. The first thing to enter my head was why go to all the fuss of having an alias if you're giving away the address where you live? I was intrigued and not only because it was Allenby. I called her room then waited in the lobby at Hertford Street for her arrival. The way she walked along the hallway reminded me of one of those catwalk models with the swagger as she put one foot in front of the other and glided through the air with a sexy sashay. I stumbled along behind her like the incredible hulk.

* * *

As we arrived at Rutland Gardens, Knightsbridge, there was a black Mercedes stopped at the porter's lodge at the entrance, waiting for the barrier to be lifted, and that's when I first saw Susan Barrett. If Gabriella was the Angelina Jolie type then the woman in the car was a blonde-haired Sharon Stone clone and she certainly caught my attention. I was out of the cab in a flash and at the open Mercedes window.

"Hi, am I dreaming or have we met before? I'm Bobby Brown and you must be Superwoman. Would you mind if I just stood here and gazed for a while?" It was my usual line. It never worked, but hell, what's a man to do if not try? I was ignored.

"I'll be in number 32," she said to the gatekeeper without even a smile in my direction.

"Right you are, madam," he replied as the gate rose and she started to move forward without bothering to notice me.

It was a private conversation meant to have no significance beyond the driver and the gatekeeper. They were wrong. Number 32 was where I was to escort Gabriella. I wouldn't leave it alone. Stupid is as stupid does. As the car window began to close, I shouted,

"Tell him Bobby was outside with Gabriella. Tell him to have fun and I'll see him later at the club."

I walked Gabriella to the elevators and waited for her to rise to the top floor, paying no attention to the fact that I had forgotten one of Mr Henry's rules as set out at our first meeting such a long time ago.

* * *

"I will have to make room for your talents, Tom. Considerable as they are, they are not what I'm short of. I shall put you in charge of special thing which up till now has not been done to my satisfaction." He was standing at the drinks cabinet looking every inch the nasty person he was. The air in the pokey office room was full of his cigar smoke and the pungent smell of his aftershave with a heavy fragrance of menthol, was trying to break through the fog. From a room off to the side of his office I could faintly hear the gravelly voice of Mick Jagger's rendition of *Route 66* and the memory of that story I'd heard of *Jumping Jack* flashed unobstructed into my mind.

"One thing here we don't do is get involved with what our clients get up to in the comfort of their own homes, Tom. Our business is here in the club. What goes on outside is not of our concern," he was shaking his head.

"People who use our facilities don't like their recreations known to all and sundry. They like to keep their affairs quiet and private and that's what they pay for. It could be a sex thing, or a reliance on drugs, or a gambling blemish, but their foibles, whatever they may be, are their own to share or not with those next to their heart or their wallet, as the case may be. I do so like that word, foibles, it reminds me of something. But there I go, off on one again. You do understand all that I've been saying don't you, Bobby? That's the name you start with here; Bobby Brown. Go on then. Go get accustomed to all your new surroundings, Bobby Brown. I hope you find them much better than a prison cell. Keep yourself busy in the foyer and the bar tonight, putting the names to the faces." At that he dismissed me, allowing just two words of thanks to leave my lips before he too left towards the sound of *Ruby Tuesday* playing in that distant room.

* * *

Many years had past since that initiation and here I was back in that same smoke filled office of his. He was pouring his second glass of Scotch when we arrived at what I had withheld. He offered me a refill, but I refused. I wanted to get out of the room as soon as I could with my foibles still my own.

"It is important, vital even, that only I know all there is to know, Bobby. There are some influential clients amongst our punters both here below and in our other establishments, that give us their trust. If their partialities were to become public knowledge they would probably stop their association with me. That would mean cuts, Bobby, and I don't necessary mean simple redundancies. Are you still following?" His eyes had never left me throughout this insight and although I wanted to look away, I couldn't.

"If I thought you were holding something back, some knowledge you have of activities beyond these walls that I am not aware of, I would have no alternative but to chop your balls off, Bobby."

"I would share everything I know with you, boss," I replied defiantly but suspecting he had something up his sleeve. It didn't take long to discover what that was.

* * *

Having drawn a blank with the delicious looking woman in the car, I was about to return to the cab and collect Gabriella, simply chalking it up to her misfortune, but as she drove through the gate I clocked the personalised number plate; ED1T. It didn't take a genius to trace the owner. If Alice had been aware of this she may have approved as I hadn't lied to Mr Henry, but I hadn't told the truth either.

* * *

"Bobby, you have disappointed me. I know about you taking a girl to Marcus Allenby's address and then speaking to Phillip Barrett's wife. However, at this stage slicing your undercarriage away could be rather unwise considering how much trouble Allenby has caused me. Perhaps, and I'm not trying to put words in your mouth, your reason behind addressing the woman in question was to find information about Allenby. Hmm?" He asked, pretending he was bemused. Somehow I was able to keep the relief I felt inside rather than emit the loudest exhalation possible.

"You've got it there, boss. And I did find out some stuff. I was holding back in case I could put more to it as time went on. I didn't want to bring only snippets of gossip to your door. If I had known that you already knew of Gabriella then I would have told you earlier, but there's not a lot yet." As the word, 'snippets' left my mouth I wondered as to its suitability.

"Go on then, join the dots up for me on what you've got, Bobby, and be the good boy I know you can be."

This time I did sigh but I disguised it from being a sigh of rescue to a sigh of agitation. I told him all that I'd found out about Susan Barrett and then, without knowing it, I crossed over the same path my sister had walked. Although I didn't know of course that she had carried a camera.

"Allenby married Phillip Barrett's best friend's younger sister, Patsy Tomlinson, boss."

"Did he! When did that happen?" His knuckles turned white as he held the arms of chair to stop himself jumping down my throat when I told him that.

"I'm not sure, boss. Found out about it by listening in to a conversation Tomlinson and Barrett were having."

"But roughly how long ago? Was it months or years, Bob?" He stifled the agitation he was feeling by gripping harder.

"Months if not less, boss."

"You say Barrett's wife works in the print, Bobby?"

"She's the editor of *The Courier*, boss."

"Does she know her husband's bent?"

"I wouldn't know the answer to that one, Mr Henry."

* * *

It was only in her deepest moments of despair that Susan allowed herself to feel the shame about how her life had evolved, and that was not as seldom as one might think. On the one hand she admired her own composure and poise when taking control of the unpleasant situations arising from her marriage, but despised herself for all that she had done in covering them up. She was addicted to the aberrant side of herself in the same manner as an alcoholic is to drink, or as a *user* is dependent upon hard drugs. In coherent moments, when her balanced mind was in control, she was depressed by her weakness and sickened by it, wanting to escape those who used her and those she used. Logic was what she wanted to avoid, just as those who drink to forget or have become reliant on their own form of drug do not want to live in the cruel world that reality shows them every day. Sex was her evasion from all that had hurt in the past and her way of avoiding attachments to actualities. The men and women that she used in her freakish pursuits were contained in a box marked pleasure, full of random, empty people with none of the substance that Mary had referred to. There was one box she longed to fill that had remained empty throughout her adult years. Love was its name and to her it was the sweet that was furthest from her reach, always above the candy and the sugary ones on which she satiated regularly.

Both her journalist parents had been drinkers. It was the fashion then, as was staying in marriages that were shams at best and battlegrounds at worst.

Theirs had been a bit of both, with the adolescent Susan learning quickly how to get out of the way of flying crockery and threats. In her conscious memory, normal was making and doing everything for herself, meals, laundry, shopping and finding out the facts of life. There had never been someone to turn to for affection or guidance or to help her along life's path. Only two pugnacious parents driving her onwards towards a goal that they wanted for her.

The drunken arguments were always violent and Jeremy, Susan's father, had not come by the nickname of 'bruiser' by default, it had come by way of Susan's mother's fists. Sophie was a big woman in temper and size and when the drink-infused brawls ended she was always the last standing with Jerry either lying or grovelling at her feet. Whether it was the act of physical violence inflicted on him, or the fact that he was never what Susan imagined a father figure to be, that shaped her into what she became, only she would be able to tell you, but this much I'm sure of, she saw something in Phillip that she coveted above all else.

Sad to say, their marriage was short-lived. It was never the type of closeness to last the lifetime that Susan desired more than anything. For him it was a distraction and statutory, maybe there was pleasure to some extent in the beginning, but, if so, it was a dangerous and unpredictable pleasure, one where he was never in charge. Things changed when he met Allan

Tomlinson. Tomlinson was accustomed to being in control of matters, be they in his personal life or in his professional one. He had never married and was unused to compromise. Tomlinson was always the Alpha and the Omega. Phillip was neither, relying on Susan to find the end to what she had started. To her, Phillip was the subservient participant she wanted, but not the lover she needed. The sexual pleasures he sought, both in and away from marriage, he had, but not a male lover domineering him. It wasn't long before he began to bore her with one excuse after another until finally she realised there was nothing left in her box of tricks appealing enough for him.

She hated moments on her own when the glimmer of what she should have become shone through above the sleaziness of her vacuous life. When hesitation and withdrawal were her only companions there was nobody she could turn to and assist in her ineffectual resolve. She was lonely in a normal world and hated it. Hating herself for wanting to live there and despising her weakness for remaining. When the Barrett's divorced Susan slithered sideways into Phillip's son's life. Rupert luxuriated beneath her stiletto heels, leather costumes and assertive demands, whilst his father dug deeper into his pockets for his honour to remain unblemished.

Part Eight

Gabriella described nothing to me of her visit to Marcus Allenby in Rutland Gardens, nonetheless, she agreed to tell Mr Henry everything. Apparently it was his money which did the persuading, or so she told me when we next saw each other at the house in Hertford Street. I had learned early in life that money was a precious commodity never to be wasted whatever the circumstances. Perhaps that lesson came on the day of our father's death because that day has remained solidly in my memory when other memories have faded. Despite having only a few recollections of our parents, it is conspicuous that I inherited none of my mother's good-natured qualities which seemed to have been bestowed on Alice. However, I did take after her in regard to the safekeeping of money. It follows that I got the rest of my psyche from our father, and to that I must say that he must have been one hell of a stupid bastard.

He had died suddenly when working on a diesel locomotive in the repair yards at London Bridge Station. There was no commotion at home or floods of tears, only four burly men of a variety of shape and size all crowded into our back room with grease stained hands being busily wiped by oil blacken cloths. He always had the same, our father that is, hands that were never white no matter how long he stood at the kitchen sink scrubbing at them. Mum was making tea, and a packet of biscuits had been found, something I didn't know we possessed. Neither Alice nor I were big eaters, but I remember Alice looking at me with ravenous intentions on seeing those chocolate covered biscuits. I made straight for them, not wanting to share with her or anyone.

"They're not for you two, they're for your dad's mates," Mother said, as her work-hardened hand found the back of my head but not Alice's.

"They've come for the Christmas Club money. I can't find it, it's not in the jar next to the book. Look; there's only small change and one ten-shilling note." The emptied tin of Bird's Custard Powder with its remnants was ceremoniously displayed and then discarded to the sink top.

"Do you know where else he might have kept it?" She asked me as though I was included in dad's deceit.

"I don't like to say this," she said looking into the centre of the group of four. "But you might be better off asking if he left it in the bookies up the road.

He's always in there," then sombrely adding. "when he was alive."

Apparently he was a renowned gambler, so Mum had surprisingly told, unbeknown to his long-suffering mates still wringing those dirty hands, still waiting in frustration with symptoms of worry exchanged from one dirty faces to another. Mum stood, head bowed, facing the bare floor as the men gathered in a circle, mumbling and shaking their heads. As Alice and I looked in every cupboard I saw Mum's trembling hands making more tea and handing the biscuits around; again.

We looked all through our home until at last all possible hiding places had been searched and no monies, be they marked Christmas, Easter or any other kind found. She had no explanation other than the one she had offered, adding how foolish they had been in entrusting her husband with the responsibility in the first place. She suggested calling in the police, but to what avail, she asked.

"He's dead. The poor sod can't be punished anymore, can you? But you can punish me and my kids. Word will get around soon enough that he was a thief without the rozzers knocking on my street door adding more shame and grief to this household on this day. Haven't we had enough? It's not the children's fault, is it?" she implored, pointing at us two kids. She was good, my mum; even I believed her.

The four imprudent men left with no words of consolation for mum, only empty diesel oil sullied hands that were clutching air and not the expected four thousand eight hundred and forty-five pounds that the twenty-three railway engineers had handed over in weekly instalments to our departed father. I knew what a club was but wondered what Christmas money looked like, imagining it to be the sort wrapped in gold and tasting of chocolate until sensible Alice put me straight.

"Dad must have bet it away then, although I never knew he liked the horses, did you, Tom?" she asked pointlessly, as I had no idea what either Dad or Mum liked or didn't come to that.

That Christmas, three weeks after he died, both Alice and I were given sweets as presents. That's probably why I remember all of it so well. Normally at Christmas new school clothes were the only presents we were given and that was dependent on if, or how much, we had grown. The next unusual event was when the rented television was exchanged for a bigger model when there was nothing wrong with the old one. Then the tally man stopped calling for his weekly subscriptions towards the debt our parents had accrued. Mum told everyone, including us, that it was Dad's life insurance money that paid it off and everyone except me believed it. My opinion of my dad changed suddenly; he had become a stooped Robin Hood providing what our mother called 'her tuppence ha'penny' she had on the side. I inherited the dishonesty both my parents possessed, but the only saving club I contributed into was safely locked away in the basement of London Wall House.

* * *

When Mr Henry had calmed down from my unexpected introduction of Allan Tomlinson into our conversation. After offering me a drink he explained how Marcus Allenby had induced the transfer of ownership of the club and why Tomlinson had arranged his sister's wedding. It centred around the huge amounts of money Henry owed because of the incautious dealings Allenby had conducted.

"The debt was refinanced through an off-shore company structured by my financial advisor many years ago. That saved most of my real estate having to be sold or the likelihood of me being declared bankrupt. Phillip Barrett used his son's name, Rupert, to front-up a consortium that paid part of the price for my business interests in cash money with both Marcus Allenby and Allan Tomlinson in overall control, but not named as directors. It was Tomlinson who raised the majority of the money to finance the deal. Patsy Tomlinson is the pawn in the middle of it all. She's a drunk and a heroin addict. She's had too much money and spare time on her hands all her life and chose the wrong path to go down. Her mother liked a drink for sure, but this one is way off the rails. I'm betting that Marcus is unaware of the actual reason behind it all. All he can see is Patsy's money waving at him. I believe it's Tomlinson's way of making sure the family fortune falls into his own lap. But I'm in a position to make sure that won't happen. Things are about to be changed a wee bit."

I refilled both his and my own glass and accepted a cigar from the polished black inlaid cigar box that he pushed across the desk in my direction. I lit it and waited for him to continue.

"According to my legal brief there's a family will that leaves the entire Tomlinson estate to the surviving relative if anything happens to either Patsy or Allan Tomlinson. That estate is worth close on five billion pounds, Bobby! Neither of them had children, so they're the last. Allan Tomlinson will be the only beneficiary when his sister pops her clogs, and if he's cute, and I think he is, he can drop Marcus into the frame for murder, or at least manslaughter. Patsy Tomlinson is many things, but a willing participant in the games that Allenby likes to play she is not. She suffers from a severe lack of confidence and self-assurance. Basically she hates herself. She used to cut herself when she was young. Terrible to see, that was," he shook his head in disbelief then carried on with his appraisal.

"Getting her involved in his filthy games will end her. She will hate herself even more than she does now. Her drugged up mind won't cope with all of that. I reckon she will take an overdose and that's what Tomlinson is hoping. He owes millions and he hasn't got it and the only way he can get it is if his sister dies. He wants a fast end without getting his hands dirty. He can say that he didn't know about Allenby's immoral ways. A good brief will get him away with that. He will then say that if he known about that side of Allenby, he would have told his sister not to marry. Marcus knows of Patsy dependency and her previous addiction to self-abuse leading to the depression she suffers from, and Allan Tomlinson can prove he knows. When she goes, and I don't believe that will be far off, Tomlinson could say Allenby forced his sister's acquiescence into his bizarre pastimes with the sole intention of killing her and thereby inheriting her money."

"I know this business, girls, gambling and what have you, better than anyone but show me a corporation document or an order of transfer of interest and I'm lost. Sir Giles Milton QC is the best that money can buy. It was he who told me of the will and I took his advice over this deal. I'm staying on running affairs until I decide to go. That gives me plenty of scope to rock all their boats. I want you to go see this Susan Barrett and tell her that her ex-husband has been photographed having sex with unnamed men in a club in Liverpool that the local council wanted closed but he allowed to be kept open. I have the evidence in full. There's also a photograph of him accepting a big fat brown envelope from a man whose face has been obscured. I have the original with the man's face as clear as crystal along with a statement of his saying how much is in the envelope. If she says that she doesn't care what her ex gets up to in his spare time show her this, Bob. It should swing it my way."

By now it wasn't just the fact that the office had no air-conditioning, as was evident by the increasing sweat rolling down from my forehead or sliding down my back, it was also fear of what he was going to ask me to do. I looked at the coloured photograph he pushed across the desk towards me. As I was looking he picked up a pile of photos and came to stand beside where I sat. He slowly put one after another before me whilst steadying himself on my shoulder.

"You won't know the third woman in these. That's Patsy Tomlinson, and whatever Susan Barrett is doing with that thing in her hand looks completely unnatural to me, but if ever I'm invited to a police college to give a lecture on how to utilise equipment I'll show them just how versatile a truncheon can be. Could be quite *invigorating* for some of them. By the look on Gabriella's face when it's her turn to have that thing poked into her, it looks a mite uncomfortable, wouldn't you say. As I said, Bobby, I know this trade inside out. You might have more muscles than the average person but I'm way ahead in any intelligence contest. What surprised me the most about that meeting you took Gabriella to, is that you never put a camera in her bag to take to Rutland Gardens." He was right, I had lots to learn.

"Unless Susan Barrett, or whatever she's calling herself nowadays, does what I've written in this envelope I'll post some selective snaps of her to *The Sun* newspaper and a couple of the other rags. They might well like to print what the editor of a rival newspaper gets up to when not commenting on the absence of morals in the lives of prominent people. Make sure you tell her that, Bobby." He pushed harder on my shoulder when he placed the sealed envelope next to me picking up a photograph as he did so.

"Weird angles that Marcus can distort his body into when the editor lady is whipping him. Strange what people like."

"Help yourself to the booze and take a cigar with you when you go. I'm off to take my mid-morning tablets then have a lay down for an hour or so. I must be getting too old for all this excitement. See yourself out and don't forget to put the photos in the envelope and take it with you. Oh, and by the way," he said, pressing harder as he stood.

"Don't fuck with me again, Bobby Brown. It's the second time it's worked in your favour. Don't try for a third, son, or I'll be buying a headstone with Tom Collins written on it."

* * *

Patsy took her own life when finally the sham of a marriage to Marcus became more odious and insufferable than her drinking and heroin could cope with. As it happened on the day after photographs of her husband's predilection for abnormal sexual habits were blazoned across newsstands, one can only assume that was her tipping point. Mr Henry had been right in his estimation of Patsy's mental state of mind.

***

"It's you or me, Marcus, and it ain't going to be me flushed down the toilet!" Those were Susan's parting words to Allenby as she replaced one telephone receiver then picked up another to the print room, telling them to run with the story that led to Patsy's suicide.

"What did the man who showed you those photographs look like, Susan?" Marcus had asked when she'd rung and the threat trickled down his ears.

"Flat busted nose, yellowy red hair and built like Arnold Schwarzenegger, only a lot taller."

"And what's stopping me naming you as the masked woman in the photo?" he followed his first question with another.

"Three things really; one, I can't be recognised. Two, I can't be recognised, and three, I'll sue you for every penny you've got. Now take your punishment and be quiet about it. It will blow over in a week."

At thirty-four years of age Marcus Allenby possessed the same *l'amour de la vie* that he found encapsulated within his innermost gatherings of chic associates on the outskirts of Saint-Tropez. It had been there that Patsy and he had met. She was a vivacious thirty-three-year-old. Sensually constructed and striking in appearance with hair the colour of coal and eyes as blue as the sea. She was living in her late family's chateau five miles inland. Her appetite for life matched his, with her wealth and income distracting his attention from her growing drug dependency. Happy times were shared, but in the months leading to the wedding there were more violent times than happy, when his drinking and her drugs erupted into warfare that on occasions needed the local gendarmerie to placate.

* * *

Allan Tomlinson's 'British jobs for the British' mantra when on the pollsters and extensively quoted, was never challenged by the heritage police of the other parties. Not, I doubt, because his ancestral past had not been minutely researched, but perhaps the stench of history clung to many cloaks that had been discarded whilst stepping on heads along the way to the political power so prized and fought over. If nothing else Tomlinson was a powerful ally within the walls of Westminster. His lineage had a traceable civic pedigree dating back through Britain's trading past that the country would now sooner forget than be reminded of by its former colonies. The Tomlinson hands were far from clean when it came to controversy. Where money was an issue they were a careful family. The two surviving siblings received an income from a trust fund divided unequally between them. Allan took the brunt and Patsy the not so miserable remainder. The estate stayed under legal jurisdiction until either died, when the whole package would fall under the control of the remaining offspring to do with as they were so inclined. Allan Tomlinson was about to become enormously wealthy and ripe for Mr Henry's picking, especially as candidates for the New Year's Honour List were being mooted in the press and Mr Henry had a pocketful of aces.

Hypocrite that he was, Tomlinson avoided like the plague being caught on camera wearing an Adidas or Nike motif when walking his dogs around Hyde Park, opposite his London home, just in case they had been manufactured in China or some unacceptable place. Inside his home or with friends, was another matter. Other than walking his two white Bichon dogs, he was an inactive soul not used to having his sedentary life disturbed by much. Disconcertment of any kind did not find a welcome in his household. However, he did not mind being disturbed by the Secretary to Her Majesty's Honours Committee; with the deliberations over a possible knighthood. The regular calls and lunches that the secretary and Allan participated in filled the Tomlinson diary, keeping his house attendant busy tabulating.

* * *

It wasn't Patsy's death that drove Marcus wild, that he had foreseen, and up until the moment he found out to the contrary, to be welcomed, nor was it the disgrace that the photographs caused him. What did was the fact that now he had no influence over his wife's cauldron of money. On that discovery, he telephoned Allan Tomlinson expressing in explicit depth his acute anger over his inability to access funds, suggesting that the two meet and come to an arrangement in Marcus's favour, very quickly before his temper deteriorated and the situation was unalterable. Anxiety joined hands with apprehension sending Tomlinson to scythe down all before him on his rapid way to Phillip Barrett's door.

Phillip Barrett was a man who did not fit his clothes. It was not intentional nor done as an act of protest, it was purely an accident of shape. No matter how his tailor fitted his suit or cut his shirt, they hung shabbily as if in deliberate defiance of convention. Perhaps because of this discrepancy, he was the type of man who travelled unnoticed where position in life is worn as a decoration; he simply tucked his shirt inside his trousers until the next time they separated. Allan Tomlinson was the epitome of refinement and the standard-bearer for traditional style and flair. He was a silk handkerchief in jacket breast pocket aficionado, gloss polished shoes and whenever it didn't appear too ostentatious, which was never, a full gold hunter attached to a gold Albert watch chain and a silver-topped walking cane.

It was Susan who opened the door to the flustered, unshaven and sweating Allan Tomlinson. His hair was uncombed, he wore no tie nor jacket, and one side of his trouser braces was unbuckled and allowed to hang freely.

"Ah, Allan, just the person I had on my list to see. Care to give me a quote on where you stand on homosexual relationships as opposed to the depravity practised by your late sister's husband? If you're staying for any length of time, could I also ask you about your love of my husband and how that has affected yours and my life?"

Tomlinson stood there visibly quivering in fear and lost for words, looking over Susan's shoulder at Phillip willing him to come to his aid. Susan hadn't finished with him, but it wasn't Susan that frightened him.

"I should say I'm sorry for your loss, but as you have obviously read my lead story about Marcus Allenby in yesterday's edition it would seem as though you might be in need of a rear-guard action in the not so far off future so I won't waste my time. I do understand that will be one of the vindications Marcus Allenby may use. You know the ones—*it has been okay for Members of Parliament and local government officials for so long, I thought anything goes nowadays so I got stuck in as it were.*

"Pardon the pun there, gents. Every offence intended. I'm thinking about running a - Clean Up British High Society Campaign. What shall I print, Allan? Privileged positions? No! That might be too suggestive. How about the push to success?...Oh, I don't know. But I'll think of something to highlight the secret life of the socially advantaged and how they force compliance on their underlings. If I were to word it in a suitable fashion I could rescue Mr Barrett senior's good name and reputation," she paused, "No! I won't do that either." She stated, staring hard at Phillip with hate filled eyes boring into him, before turning back to Tomlinson.

"I do intend to save my accusation that it was your threats towards my ex that forced me to participate in anything that may be discovered by other newspaper editors. My mind was perverted by you two. Are you getting that uncomfortable feeling that people are ganging up against you, Allan? Care to give me an off-the-cuff quote, or would you rather I ad-lib on your behalf?"

"Your friend Marcus Allenby has been on the telephone threatening to kill me in a hundred of repugnant ways, Madam. I need your ex-husband's help and then I need the police" he pleaded, almost in tears. Susan and Phillip looked at each other, neither rushing for their telephones.

Tomlinson's distressed state did not end at the Barrett's door. When presentably calm and collected, he returned to his Hyde Park Gardens home finding a business card awaiting him on the hall stand. An invitation to meet - a concerned member of the former Kiss Club.

I would be grateful if you would meet me on Sunday at 2:30pm in The Soho House, Dean Street to discuss a matter of interest regarding the Kiss Club.
It was signed—Harry Henry.

Part Nine

The relationship between my sister and Sir Giles Milton flowed effortlessly from inception to ordination. Passing restraint to obsession, from lust to passion and finally arriving at love. An intimacy and adoration shared by both. Months passed, with Alice spent in oblivion to everything other than the man she loved, until she was reminded of those headlines about Marcus Allenby's fondness of iniquity.

"You know I knew him once."

"Who?" Giles asked as the two of them lay in his bed on the third floor at Cheyne Walk.

"Did you know that you have fewer steps than I have to get to bed? There are forty-three to the top floor at Charterhouse Square and only thirty-four to your bedroom. That's why we should only have sex in bed at my place. You would get more exercise that way."

"What are you talking about, Alicia? You're not making a lot of sense."

It was a lazy Sunday morning when everyone had forgotten about the suicide of Patsy Allenby/Tomlinson. Time had passed and different headlines took centre spot in newspapers.

"Marcus Allenby! I met him with Susan Barrett the editor of *The Courier* at my Red Spiky George exhibition. He bought tons of what I had on display that night. She was with her husband, but she knew him all right. I reckon they were either sleeping together or had been and not long parted. I thought it strange that she led the witch hunt for his head. At the time I thought that maybe they'd had one almighty row and it was her way of getting her own back. You know the saying - a woman scorned and all that. But it was a horrendous thing to do if that was the reason. There's an article in the Sunday supplement about her and it brought it all back. She's divorced now. Gone back to her maiden name; Rawlinson. But it's her. No doubt about that. She's a striking woman."

"What's the article all about then?" Giles asked as he lazily reached across to see the picture.

"Dreams. Apparently she wrote a book on the subject that was quite successful. In her new one she's staying with the same subject, only using Lewis Carroll's *Alice's Adventures in Wonderland* as an example and going to speak about dreams at the Barbican Centre. According to this article Rawlinson is quite an accomplished speaker. The interesting thing from your perspective is that your fishing companion, Dr Colin Princely is on the bill. He's giving a chat on neurological diseases and their psychiatric manifestations. It's in two weeks' time. Feel like going and falling asleep?"

"Or worse coming out as a psychopath and murdering the both of them. That wouldn't be fair in Colin's case though, but perfectly in order for her," he remarked unguardedly.

"What do you mean by that, do you know this woman, Rawlinson?" Alice asked.

"It's just that I've heard some stories about her and didn't like what I heard. But what's all that got to do with Marcus Allenby?" he hastily added as an afterthought.

"Nothing. It was just seeing Susan's name reminded me of him. Now give me all the sordid bits that Mary would have told me had she been here and not working so hard in Switzerland once again. I worry about her, you know.

"I know you do, but she's a big girl, Alicia. She can look after herself. Don't worry so much or you'll get lines across your forehead." He lay on his side and gently stroked her face.

"Don't get too far in front of yourself. I'm waiting on the sordid bits, Giles," she said as she nudged him in the side with her elbow.

"It's been a few years since I heard those rumours, she's probably changed by now. Anyway it's only hearsay and I don't deal with conjecture. Best left alone after all this time. Let the devil lie where it is," he replied pompously.

"That's a strange phrase, where did that come from, Gilly?"

He never elaborated on her question, allowing the situation of a warm bed and two amorous occupants to take hold in the anticipation of mutual satisfaction to dispel her curiosity. My sister's interest did not reach further than that article. It stopped when Giles started. Had she kept reading she would have seen that Susan was the exponent of a campaign for - Women Who Suffer From Abuse - 'Is there nothing that this cost cutting government can do for the defenceless women of this country?' Her facts were wrong and her innuendos were strong but market penetration was the influence behind it, not the unnecessary search for truth.

* * *

The sleeping lovers were disturbed by the ringing of Alice's mobile phone. It was a little after eleven o'clock in the morning. It was Mary's phone that was calling.

"Good morning, Mary! What time did you arrive home? I wasn't expecting you until Wednesday." However, it wasn't Mary who answered.

"I'm sorry to disturb you but Mary O'Donnell insisted that I call you in person. My name is Croft. I'm a resident oncologist here at Guys Hospital. Mary was admitted to the hospital on Friday. She's on Crowe Ward in the Southwark Tower, sixth floor, and it would be wise if you could come now." The connection died as Alice sprang alive.

* * *

The memories came flooding back in waves of regret as Alice manoeuvred through the many roadworks from Chelsea to London Bridge with her fingers crossed and in silent prayer for her friend.

"I want us to befriend a homeless child, Mary. I don't mean foster or adopt or anything formal like that, just to be their friend in the outside world. It means visiting them at the children's home and taking them out for the day or inviting them here and chilling out with them. It will give one of them a chance of getting used to being away from all the rest and interacting with people older than themselves. A first step on the way to becoming independent. What do you think?"

"What will you be doing next? Billboards tied front and back advertising the Samaritans, Alicia?" Mary laughingly asked whilst her mind and attention were firmly fixed on a client's portfolio that she needed to work on.

"Well, no, but I was thinking of volunteering for St Mungo's, the homeless charity. I want to help, Mary, to get their plight more recognisable not just ignored and swept under the carpet. After all, without you, that's where I would have ended up."

"You always forget your talent with that camera of yours when you say things like that. You would have got noticed without me. But what the hell, let's go for it. I'm in. I can't see it causing any harm and it could do some good."

As she followed an enforced diversion over Chelsea Bridge, so the memories altered shape, from charitable to insensitive and on to merciless.

Spiky George came to mind with her otherwise narrow eyes widening on receipt of the hundred pounds Alice paid for the photographs taken in her shabby hostel, and dingy room. Twenty-six were mounted for the exhibition off Piccadilly with Piccadilly prices being charged for them. Alice banked almost fourteen thousand pounds for those alone. On the drive back from the squalid to the grand, her justification for the negligible payment came from the reasoned belief of saving Georgia from the evils of drink. From out of the blue Alice had become the arbitrator on the requisites of the lifestyle of another.— *I will not pay you anything near what I shall sell the photos for because that will shorten your life.* Just how magnanimous was that? But was it? She asked herself, re-examining all that had gone before. Had Mary's kindness eaten the heart from her own benevolence?

Then there was Giles. She had accompanied him early in their relationship, when he appeared at Leeds Crown Court defending three London-based criminals accused of an armed robbery at a building society on the outskirts of the city. The only real evidence the Crown Prosecutor had, was based on identification, but as the robbers had been masked, it was open to conjecture as to its reliability. Giles was to test that speculation. They had booked a room in the centre of

Leeds instead of more touristy Harrogate on Alice's insistence of being near *city life* with her camera at the ready. What should have been a quick and easy dismissal for Giles was prolonged by the unswerving testimony of a clerk of the building society who Alice listened to from the packed public gallery. Unfortunately the evidence given by this witness had irritated Giles, and he was not about to overturn it as simply as he could have. He wanted her agony prolonged.

The police evidence was weak and inconclusive. They had found the three together in a hotel lobby, a mile from the scene, paying the overnight bill and about to leave. There was none of the stolen money on them or in any of their rooms, but there were gloves, scarves and jackets fitting the description as those worn at the robbery, all of which were readily available on any high street. The perpetrators of the crime had worn nylon stockings but none were found. Identification parades were arranged and the two cashiers who were present at the time of the robbery were given the chance to pick out the guilty. Each of the accused took part in a line-up with eight volunteer participants all dressed in identical clothing. The first of the cashiers, a man, could identify no one. He was at the furthest till point from the doorway when all three men had entered, and kept his head down as instructed. The second witness had been the one to take the full brunt of their verbal assault. She asked all eight on each of the identification parades to speak. She said she would be able to recognise the dialect used by one particular assailant. All three men had repeatedly stated that they were together at the time of the robbery but had no other alibi, so not unnaturally the police charged all three when the female witness picked out the one she said she remembered. The papers went to the Criminal Prosecution Service who, when taking into account the previous armed robbery convictions of all three, decided to prosecute knowing that the previous history was inadmissible as evidence. All rested on the woman's identification.

Giles's cross examination was cruel in its delivery and persistent in defamation.

"You are here in this court today and before this jury wishing to condemn a man, and by association two others, on your recollection of a brief, violent shouted dialogue lasting on your own admission for no more than five to seven-seconds. This was the time span your colleague has attested to and you have agreed. You have, madam, a magnificent memory."

Giles was instructed by the trial judge to rephrase his remarks into a question.

"Would I be correct in assuming that you think you have a good memory, Miss Bishop?"

"Yes! I would say that I have a fair one," she replied, confidently addressing the jury.

"Yet on the birth of four of your five children you have been unable to recall such a minor detail as the name of their father. Was it the one man or were they

all different and you did not bother to enquire as to their names?" He didn't wait for a reply.

"Over the seven-year period that those three girls and one boy were born you could not recall the name of one single father. Or did they slip your mind when it came to registration?" Impassively he stood, chin resting in the palm of his left hand, stroking his face whilst scanning the documents that lay before him, leaving the question floating in the air towards the minds of the twelve jury members.

"I don't know what the birth of my children have to do with this," she replied, not looking or feeling comfortable.

"I have the certificates here." He held the pristine copied documents spread open in his right hand, accusing her with every wave as he moved forward.

"Each column under the father's name is filled with the word - 'Unknown.' Did you not ask a name? Did not the conception of those children take longer than the seconds it would have taken to write a name?" His censorious frown lingered as he challenged each of the jury with an accusing stare.

"Nevertheless, you could not remember any names. The jury may find that somewhat strange considering your recollection of an accent spoken through a nylon mask." Another stilted pause as the judge rebuked him.

"Sir Giles, you know better than that." Giles bowed his head sufficiently to avoid further censorship.

"I put it to you, Miss Bishop, that it beggars belief how you remember so clearly a masked, gun-toting robber whilst you cringed in fear of your life, but are

not able to recall any fathers' names when it comes to your children."

Hands thrust deep into his trouser pockets with gown swept aside, back arched in a way that emphasised his full height, his dominant stance was in direct contrast to his passive witness who waited, fidgeting uneasily. Her discomfort would have no time to settle.

"If I'm missing something then please tell the jury. I'm sure they would like to share in the resurrection of your ability to be so certain of one fleeting moment of five-seconds duration and yet unclear on so many others of a presumably longer period of time." There were a few stifled smiles on some jury members' faces.

"Of course I know who they were. All of them were married, that's why I put no name down. To protect them and save the embarrassment." She shouted her response to Giles's provocative questioning.

"How thoughtful of you to sacrifice your children's possible future in saving the reputation of married men. Are you normally inclined to be so self-sacrificing and philanthropic?" Again the judge intervened, but not before Miss Bishop had blurted out a reply.

"I don't know what you mean," she awkwardly replied, confused by Giles and his strategy.

"Let me put it a different way," he said as he returned to the table where the certificates were and his assistant sat. He stooped to remove his wig replacing it with a nylon stocking pulled tightly down around his face and hair. All this was completed out of sight of the wit-

ness, the jury and the judge. Without straightening, he carried on with his cross-examination.

"There you were at the time of registering the birth of let's say - Cheryl." He carefully selected one of the accusing certificates and held it aloft, pretending to search through the other papers in front of him.

"In a quiet registration room with no distractions, but instead of truly stating the child's father you chose not to. Either, as you say, to protect a marriage, or as I say on behalf of my clients, your memory played tricks on you. Yet when threatened by men waving shotguns and shouting obscenities directly at you wearing masks similar to the one I'm now wearing, you can accurately recall a man's accent." Theatrically he turned to face the court.

"So much so that you could, without question or doubt, identify that man unequivocally. No hesitation, no second thoughts." He removed the stocking and swept his mop of black hair aside as he replaced his barrister's wig.

"Did my voice change at all whilst wearing that stocking, Miss Bishop?"

"I know what I heard," she answered defiantly.

"That was not my question, madam. I asked had my voice changed whilst I was wearing the stocking."

"Perhaps, slightly," she replied.

"The court would prefer a yes or a no to that question, Miss Bishop." He stood hands on hips as if addressing a recalcitrant teenager.

"Yes, there was a difference."

"Precisely, even I could hear a difference and I'm most certain the jury could. However, at Leeds Central Police Station although all of the participants in the identification process were asked to wear clothing similar to that worn on the robbery, none were asked to wear a stocking mask. Am I correct in that, Miss Bishop?"

"You are, yes," she said as she lowered her head fully aware of that discrepancy.

He turned the jury as he plunged his verbal knife deeper into Miss Bishop.

"Then how can the jury believe you when you say you could recognise an accent as the one spoken through a mask in the middle of a robbery when repeated to you in the quietude of a police station spoken without one? How can you be so adamant that you could not have made a mistake?"

"I don't know," she replied as she started to cry.

The judge dismissed the case without asking the jury to deliver a verdict, castigating the prosecution service for wasting the court's time and taxpayers' money. On the returning drive to their Leeds hotel Alice asked Giles if he thought the three men to be guilty of the crime as charged. He replied that he did believe they were, but when she harangued him for getting them acquitted in such a merciless fashion, he fiercely retaliated citing the incompetence of the police, not once apologising for his subversion of truth by the examination of a frightened woman.

"Good grief, Alicia! That's how I earn my money, by looking for loopholes in the truth. That's why I'm good *at my job and suitably rewarded. Barristers do not lie in court. Witnesses lie, defendants lie! Barristers for the defence avoid the truths that condemn, whilst searching the recesses of the remaining truth to find another truth that will acquit their clients. Truth has got nothing to do with justice. In a nutshell that's how the law of this country works. When the oath is taken in court it asks for the truth, the whole truth and nothing but the truth. Nowhere does it forbid another version of the truth.*

* * *

It was unabridged truth Alice found on the sixth floor of Southwark Tower at Guy's Hospital.

"This part of the hospital is closed until the morning," a fragmented voice announced as she pressed the bell on the wall at the entrance to Crowe Ward.

"I was telephoned by a consultant named Croft. A friend of mine was admitted a couple of days ago; Mary O'Donnell. It sounded urgent when he called."

"I'm sorry. Push the door when the buzzer sounds. I'm at the end of the passageway and I'll page Mr Croft for you."

The first thing Alice noticed on her walk along the hospital corridor was the lack of noise. No moans or snores from patients to disturb the silence. No wheels of moving trolleys or chairs, or the ringing of telephones. No sleeping or chatting patients in rooms leading off. In fact, no open rooms leading off. There were no nurses to be seen. Nothing moving to and fro. The eerie silence of stillness. The next sensation to hit home was the cold; it increased as she neared the end. Then came the smell. Not what she expected. Not the clean antiseptic, sharp tang in the 'staff only' escalator she had inadvertently taken instead of the public one. This was pungent and was sour. It burnt her nostrils as it travelled into her lungs. She had smelled it before; twice.

The first time was when our mother took us to the Co-Op funeral parlour to see Dad laid out in a wooden coffin on a creamy white pillow with his hair smoothed down with gel, and his face painted healthier than he'd ever been. I wondered how long it would take for the grease to show through the white gloves that he wore to his own funeral. The second time was our Mother. Bloated with the cancer that had killed her and no amount of foundation or sprayed lavender could alter that scornful smell of death that lay clasped in her crossed hands across that once wheezing chest of hers.

"Could I ask if you are a relative of Mary O'Donnell, Miss Collinson?" Mr Croft asked as he led Alice into a side waiting room away from the main corridor and where the beds should have been. It was warmer in here. She was frightened where she was. When she explained that she wasn't a relative, but the two lived together, the doctor became a little less formal.

"Alicia, wasn't it. Yes, I remember seeing your name in the mobile phone and thinking what a lovely name that was. I'm sorry it was you I had to telephone. Normally the police or social services do this but she was most insistent in asking me to tell you. I gave my word. I'm afraid your friend died twenty minutes after I called you. Perhaps I should not have said to come straight away, but there is no way of knowing in these cases how long a patient will survive. She did not suffer any pain, Alicia. I hope that helps you to know. Did your friend have any close relatives?"

Stunned, shocked, traumatised. Alice sat beside the consultant unable to focus on what he was asking for a few seconds, still thinking of the disparity between the recollections she had on the way here and the similarities she shared with Mary, yet profoundly aware of what had separated them. Now she was dead. The living distinction was dead. Separation was now absolute. The crushing news was starting to settle.

Mary is dead.

"No, she had no relatives. None whatsoever and that's why she befriended me. I was ..." Alice hesitated, sweeping a strand of hair away from her face to distract his attention from the tear forming in her eye. *What was I? She asked herself before answering the consultant's question.*

"Well, I was what I was. It doesn't seem important, but it should be. She saved my life, you know. I loved that woman, but I don't think I ever told her." It was then that she broke down and cried.

"I'll ask a nurse to come and sit with you while I fetch you a cup of tea." He said as he stood, moving the room's only decoration; a box of tissues, closer to where my sister sat with the misery.

"There is a chapel on the ground floor where you may find more solace if you are a believer in God, but you're welcome to stay here as long as want. Your friend will shortly be taken through to the mortuary before going on to the Chapel of Rest. Maybe you would prefer to say your goodbyes there."

* * *

Twenty minutes before Mr Henry left for The Soho House and his rendezvous with Tomlinson, he unlocked the top right-hand drawer of his desk and withdrew the single content; an unframed photograph of two adults, a man and a women in their thirties with two children, a boy and a baby girl held in the woman's arms. The man was square shouldered, dark haired, tanned and hard faced. He was taller than the woman. She was petite, also tanned, blonde haired, and whilst undeniably attractive appeared ill at ease, standing with a gap between her and the man. Henry rubbed his forefinger over the faces in the photograph as though he was erasing a mistake from a sheet of paper.

I cannot speculate what was on Tomlinson's mind nor whether he expected cucumber sarnies with cream scones and a nice cup of tea, but if that was what he anticipated it soon changed when Mr Henry rose from the studded, red leather chair he occupied in the uncrowded club bar to greet him.

"Ah, Tomlinson! Sit yourself down." He stood aside of the table and gestured to his guest to take the matching chair opposite his own. Tomlinson was not one to argue.

"I won't ask how you are, Tomlinson, as it's of no importance to me. What I have to say will drastically reshape whatever life you now believe you have. You're ruined! I should laugh but I won't. Do you recognise me, Allan?" Henry asked.

"I've no idea who you are, but you do appear to be rather ruffled about something with me in the mix of it," the Member of Parliament cautiously replied, sitting as far back as he could in the heavy armchair and wishing his inquisitiveness had not led him there.

A waiter appeared with a drinks menu from which Mr Henry ordered two coffees and refused the offer of dining. "We won't be troubling the chef today, Maurice." From the inside pocket of his jacket he laid the photograph he had previously been examining in front of Allan Tomlinson, with his scarred hand obscuring the picture.

"Do you want me to jog your memory with an old holiday snap of mine?" He never waited for a reply. The hand was removed to reveal a background of a bougainvillea-clad balconied house set in heavy foliage with the glimpse of a deeply blue sky visible through the sun-kissed leaves.

"Recognise the house do you, Allan? You should. Your mum and dad took you there every year. Know me now, do you?"

"Yes, I do. You were father's friend. Uncle Harry mum and I called you. It was your house in Spain. I must have been about sixteen in the picture as Patsy had just been born. If I remember correctly Father took us out there to celebrate my sister's birth. You two were close, I think?" It was not worry that now made him frown simply mere curiosity.

"Not as close as I got to your mum, Allan. Fancy a stiff drink with your real dad, old son?"

Part Ten

"What did the doctor say Mary died of, Alicia?" Giles asked when my sister had composed herself enough to call him.

"Pancreatic cancer! He was the one in charge of her treatment and they'd only met the once. Mary's private GP sent her to him on Friday morning and he admitted her straight away. All she'd done was notice that she had been losing weight. We both put that down to all her travelling and the fact that she was not eating properly. She hadn't been sick or anything. He said she had not suffered, Giles. But why did she not tell me she was in hospital instead of saying she had to rush off to Switzerland that morning?" There was a silence from both ends of the telephone. Giles was the first to speak.

"I'll meet you at Charterhouse Square where we can collect some of your things and you can move in here until you can fully comprehend what's happened. I'm so sorry, Alicia. I know how much she meant to you."

"I honestly don't know what I'm going to do now she's gone, Giles, but I do know I want to spend the night at 54. I know this will sound silly and I know I'm being sentimental and childish but that was our home and I want to relive the memories that we had there together. I realise they will be impossible to forget, nonetheless, time has a way of changing things and I just want to cling on to every word for as long as possible. I hope you can understand."

"I completely understand, my love. If you want company then call me and I'll come running."

"Will you be okay on your own?" my sister asked him.

"Of course I will, you daft thing. I have some papers to go through for a case tomorrow, but never mind about me, What about you? Will you be okay?"

"If I'm not I know where the whisky is." There was a nervous laugh to Alice's admission.

* * *

Although Alice knew most of Mary's friends and business associates, she did not know all their telephone numbers. She worried in case she would miss someone of importance that was only on the memory card in Mary's mobile, but the police would not allow her to have the phone because of some regulation regarding privacy laws. The obvious place to start the search for friends or associates was in Mary's office on the first floor at Charterhouse Square. She had never thought of venturing into this room without her now dead companion. Here was both Mary's shrine and place of torment. Hours spent huddled over files and computer screens then spinning across the floor seated in her padded 'executive' chair with a telephone in one hand and punching the air with the other in shrieks of delight when a *long-term, trade-me-out* paid off handsomely. Comfort through torture; a philosophy I shared with Mary.

The desk itself was of curved dark wood with two computers mounted near the centre and a telephone between them. It was facing into the room with a large bay curtain-less window behind. Its shutters were pinned open. There were terminals for mobile phones and other electrical appliances on top. At each end of the desk was a matching blue Tiffany glass lamp. On the right-hand side was a patterned placemat on which stood Mary's black china mug that she used for coffee or tea. It was unwashed, and Alice stared at the cold residue. On the inside rim were these words: Little Moments Make Big Days. Alice had bought it as a spontaneous gift when out shopping. Mary was fond of such platitudes and never fond of washing-up. Trying to avert her fragile emotions from the sentimental and focus on the fundamental, her eyes scanned the familiar room. Mary's clients files were stored in the two grey filing cabinets that stood against one wall, with a red and yellow soft leather chair beside them in which Alice would sit and sketch Mary on a telephone, or as her fingers glided across the computer keyboard. Against the other wall was her red velvet sofa on which sometimes she slept. Her blanket was rolled neatly on the floor at the side. It was a functional room, an airy room. It was Mary's room with nostalgia everywhere. Alice could not help but cry.

When she had steadied her nerves, and began to look through Mary's card index, she found some clients' names, but decided those were best contacted by her place of work. Then some phone numbers of colleagues she hadn't heard of and some she had. The head of the Fleet Street hedge fund department was inconsolable when Alice told him of Mary's death, offering his assistance in anything my sister wished to arrange as regards the funeral. She hadn't thought that far ahead, promising to get back to him when all of that had been settled. On deciding to commence her search into Mary's commercial life at the middle drawer of the desk, she found a sealed brown office envelope with the words: Only to be opened on my death by Alicia Collinson, formally known as Alice Collins, with Mary's beautiful, scrolled handwriting across the front. Terrified of what she saw she propelled her chair back towards the bay window, crashing into the windowsill, eyes fixed on the opened drawer as if something might fly out at her and savagely attack. She abandoned the chair and stood, tentatively reaching inside the drawer and extracting the envelope, turning it over and over frightened to hold it longer than a split-second in one position.

I should have been here to hold your hand.

How long had you known you were dying? Did you go straight from the doctor you normally see in Harley Street to Guy's, or did you come here first? Is that when you wrote this? Silent unanswerable questions appearing from nowhere and in no order, as the envelope was confined to the green blotter on the desktop sealed side upwards, daring not to read the 'Opened in death' bit again.

Were you crying when you wrote this?

I left for Chelsea early on Friday morning. You were in the kitchen. What made you go to see your Doctor? Did you feel unwell? What time did you see Dr Croft and where did you see him? Did you suspect he would say what he did? Did you write this before you saw any doctor?

I wish I'd told you that I loved you, Mary.

Alice pushed the brown offending envelope to one side half hoping it would disappear, saving her the task of opening it. She took May's mug to the kitchen, washed and dried it, making a coffee for herself knowing all the time that the revelation was only being delayed, but at least it was being delayed. Other than the sink, she managed to steer clear of the memory-laden kitchen appliances and retentive cupboards, and up the flight of stairs she trudged on shaking legs with trembling fingers. The first thing she saw was the envelope. Her eyes would leave it as she sat.

Were you frightened and did you want to run away?

There were only two files in the left-hand top drawer. One marked Personal, and one, Expenses. The second she thumbed through first. It contained what was on the front. Taxi receipts, restaurant bills, a few dry-cleaning invoices, petrol receipts along with some sundry items that could be examined in the future. In the one marked Personal, were papers detailing Mary's various investments and her day-to-day banking accounts. It was in the second drawer down that Alice found an additional portal into Mary O'Donnell's past life. A collection of brightly decorated birthday cards.

From the narrow cardboard box containing the cards, she withdrew a plastic folder and spread its contents on the desk in front of her. All were the same. On the front cover of each was a picture of a golden-haired girl hanging on to a balloon and smiling as she floated towards a beaming sun, waving a banner with - HAPPY BIRTHDAY as its message in sparkling letters across the top. Inside Mary had added a date to each one with the words, 'I'm so sorry, Lizzy'. There were thirty cards in all, with twenty-two signed ones. The first was dated 16/8/1994, exactly eighteen years to the day when Alice and Mary met in that bar in Bishopsgate.

So that's why you were drinking and smoking so heavily when I met you and not just as you said the markets had closed and you fancied an early lunch. Why didn't you say it would have been Lizzy's eigh-

teenth birthday. Why have you never said a word about it being the anniversary of the abortion of your child?

The anger of the dumb for being thoughtless now held hands with sadness.

The tiny tear droplets started in the corners, nearest her nose and as she again looked at the sealed envelope with its message of death they quickly filled the whole of her eyes and just would not stop. She swept the hair from the sides of her face, and with both hands grasping her head she rested her elbows on the desk blotter, and permitted her tears to fall where Mary once worked. Doubt accompanied loneliness into the room and sat beside her.

Why did I never ask if your child had a name?

* * *

In the bar at The Soho House Allan Tomlinson was sweating slightly and not just because of the heat. He held Mr Henry's photograph tightly between his forefinger and thumb of his right hand but wasn't looking at it. His gaze fell on Henry's scarred hand.

"Nasty scar that," Tomlinson said trying to ease the tension that was gnawing at his stomach lining.

"Knife did that. A bullet did this one," Henry said as he pointed at the deep depression above his eye.

"Douglas thought I was dead when he shot me, but as you can see I didn't die that easily. It came out at the side. Here," he passed his fingers through the hair above his ear, raising it higher to partially reveal the exit wound. An ugly zigzagged line of scarred tissue that disappeared higher up.

"Have you ever wondered about that boating accident of his, Allan? Never did find the body, did they. Shame really, don't you think. Especially as your mother's body was never found either. It must have been very distressing for you and your sister to lose both parents so close together and have no bodies to grieve over. I have no idea where Douglas buried your mother, but I could tell you roughly where his body might be, although I doubt there would be anything left after this amount of time. Fish are about as selective as pigs when it comes to food," Henry shrugged his shoulders in disinterest.

"Did you kill him?" The photograph began to wobble in Tomlinson's unsteady hand as he asked.

"Me, kill him? Where did that idea come from? I'm not a violent man, Allan." Henry replied, sniggering. "It was just something I was told. Why would I want to kill my best friend? He didn't mean to shoot me in the head and put me in the boot of his car then drive to Epping Forest. And it was a sheer accident that he left me in a hole he'd found by chance? It was all a bit of a game cos he was clumsy on purpose filling in the hole. What reason would I have to kill good old Douglas Tomlinson? Incidentally, Allan, you obviously never heard me a minute ago. He was not your dad, I'm your dad."

Allan Tomlinson had heard and had tried to control the reverberating sound of Henry's announcement to no avail. He couldn't imagine what damage this exposure could cause, but he did know it would cause damage. His heart had not stopped from racing since that moment, but he didn't panic, even though the news would shatter the tranquil life of a rising political star. Calmly he rested in his chair, replacing the photograph in front of Mr Henry, then studied Henry's expression for an explanation. There was none instantly forthcoming. Instead Mr Henry summoned his waiter and asked to sign the club bill, adding, "My son here has some reading material to look through that might take a while. It's some shocking news from a distant relative. If he wants anything to drink or nibble on charge it to me, please, Maurice, but don't let him buy the club using my account, will you. Tea and bites only. That okay with you, Allan?" He and Maurice, the waiter, laughed moderately whilst poor Allan was watching his knighthood sail down the Thames and into the North Sea.

From the same pocket that had held the photograph, Mr Henry withdrew some sandy coloured sheets of paper, clipped together. He placed them in the middle of the round table. When Maurice left, he spoke.

"The first of this little lot is a DNA report that Douglas commissioned when I told him about me and your mother. He was a little upset at the time. I think it was this report that made him want to kill me after he'd shot your mum. Inside it tells all you need to know about me being your biological father.

There are copies that I hold, also some sworn statements taken by a barrister friend of mine detailing some of the disgusting arrangements you have with a certain agency that deals with male prostitution. I won't lower myself by detailing the ages of the boys you used, nor will I mention the sites you view for the pornography that so enthrals you.

"If you think I'm about to blackmail you, then think again, Allan, old son. I have no need of Tomlinson money and as you're not a Tomlinson, legally you have no claim to the family estate. I'm just after ruining you and Marcus Allenby for what you tried to do to me. I'm off to a good start, aren't I! Having the degenerate son of a Soho gangster on the government front bench should go down well with your constituents and fellow party members. Have a splendid afternoon tearing your brains out thinking of the shame that's about to fall on your head. However, you can limit the damage a bit, son. I'm not all bad.

"I've written some instructions, that if you follow to the letter then I will not persecute you as much as I could. Oh, and if you have any integrity left, Allan, well, I won't mentioned a soldier's honour. Particularly what a Japanese officer might do in your position. Don't be doing anything as brave as that, or they might name some medical institute after you, especially on receipt of your donation to the charity I've suggested in those instructions. I'll leave it there and not damage the day any more than I already have." He rose from his soft armchair and stood, buttoning his jacket as he did so. The bill arrived and he signed it.

"A lot depends on what you do next, son. I'm off to phone a newspaper editor that you and I know. All of this could make tomorrow's headlines at a push. But no, I won't rush into anything. I'll give it until the morning and see what's happened."

Mr Henry took a relaxed walk to where I was waiting for him.

"Did you get her home phone number, Bobby?"

"I did, boss. Here, it's written on this card."

"You do know that Marcus will be coming after you and me, don't you, Bob?"

"I figured as much, Mr Henry. Did you want me to park up inside the club for a while, until it dies down a bit?"

"No, Bob! That won't be necessary. I don't think it will die down. I think it's just about to get very hectic. I don't need you at the club, but I do have a need of you elsewhere this afternoon. Get yourself over to Hyde Park Gardens. It's a posh private road north of Hyde Park, close to Lancaster Gate. There's a pretty garden opposite that runs the whole length of the houses. I want you walking up and down the road by those gardens, smoking a few cigarettes looking mean and threatening near number 24. When questioned, and you will be, say you're minding your own business smelling the roses and tell 'em to eff off. When Old Bill turns up, quote the European Bill of Human Rights. Won't do yer no good, but it will make the neighbours take a bit of notice. Don't go thumping anyone, Bobby. Save that for another day. Be on your best behaviour."

Mr Henry then called Susan Rawlinson.

"Ah, Susan! I understand that you were once married to Phillip Barrett, the bent civil servant who swings both ways when it comes to sex as you do yourself."

"Who are you?" she asked in an untroubled voice.

"I'm an admirer of yours, Susan. I loved that exposé of Marcus Allenby you wrote in *The Courier*. Very public spirited. That kind of sex needs to be denounced as you did. I too have a propensity for unmasking the wrongs of life. I have some interesting information on a very close friend of your ex-husband. A respected Member of Parliament, down on his luck at the moment. A certain Allan Tomlinson. Know him, do you?"

"You're the man who owns the Kiss Club in Dean Street that they've all used. You were behind those photographs."

"How very astute you are, Susan, got it in one. I thought that word, *unmasking* would give me away. I hope you are appreciative of how I kept your name a secret when it came to the woman in the mask and the leather get-up. Nevertheless, purely in my own interests I have some snaps showing a very distinctive tattoo on your right buttock. You looked in considerable pain when that one was snapped. Despite all that, I've always considered that whatever goes on behind closed doors should remain there; unless of course it's a moral issue of some national importance as in Allenby's case. However, you and I need to move further along the food chain, at least for now." He stopped speaking, removed the phone from his ear and placed it alongside a small tape recorder.

This country is being overrun by murderers, rapists and child molesters all allowed to settle here by previous governments who failed to run proper checks on their status. We are becoming the dustbin of Europe through our benefits system that is being abused by immigrants.

"That was Allan Tomlinson, Susan, a chap who preaches a holier-than-thou message yet follows a different path in his personal life. Did you know he uses young boys for his sexual gratification? All under age. Why, of course you didn't, otherwise you would have exposed the right-wing fascist. I would have thought if that information was made public then it would reflect rather badly on his love-mate Phillip Barrett, and as a consequence of you two being once married, on you. That is unless of course it can be spun around a bit so that you can come away as an innocent victim smelling of violets."

"I'm obviously not committing myself to anything conducted on the telephone, but carry on. You have my ear," Susan coyly replied.

"As long as I have that then I have your attention." Henry paused for a moment then continued in a slower more deliberate manner.

"I can, and will, supply you with enough material to destroy Allan Tomlinson's political career and personal life, confining him to a bad memory on the Tory Party's bulletin board that will leave a stain of discomfort for a lifetime. Apart from photography I have another hobby in life, Susan; I not only collect people but I discard some of them when they've served my purpose. I wish to unload Tomlinson and add you to my prestigious collection in his place, that way you can rely on me keep your little tattooed secret for as long as you play ball. Do we have an understanding?"

"I don't seem to have a way of saying no."

"Sensible lady! I have always found the print-trade to be a pragmatic organisation. I will meet you tomorrow morning in the bar at the Mayfair Hotel where we can exchange what I have and what I will require from you. I'm not a greedy man, Susan, so I shall not be expecting much. Shall we say eleven-thirty?"

Part Eleven

"I've found an envelope that I don't want to open on my own, Giles. I think it is Mary's will."

"Bring it here with you, Alicia and we're open it together. How are feeling?"

"I'm okay if I keep myself busy. I have just one more person to ring; Susan Rawlinson. I never did ask Mary about her. It's so weird how we were talking about her when the hospital rang? I wonder how she, Mary and that Marcus Allenby all met?"

"Somethings are best undisturbed, particularly when it's a one-sided disclosure. She could say anything and there's no one who could repudiate her statement. Was there anything in Mary's private papers that relates to a family she may have that you did not know of?" he asked.

"No, nothing, Giles!" She didn't know why she kept Mary's Lizzy a secret, it just seemed the right thing to do.

"Why would Susan make something up about Mary, Giles? No, that doesn't sound right. After all, Mary wouldn't have invited her to my exhibition if she never liked the woman."

"If that's the case then it follows she liked the man Susan warned you against. Perhaps Mary and this Marcus were lovers, Alicia, and this Susan was jealous. She wouldn't admit to that. She'd probably fabricate an answer and you would be none the wiser."

"Hmm, yeah, that could be right." Alice sighed before continuing, "I'll simply inform her of Mary's death and leave it there. As soon as I've done that I'll drive over. I'll bring that envelope and you can tell me what I'm supposed to do with it." She pressed—end call, on her mobile phone then looked up Susan's number.

* * *

To Alice, Susan appeared preoccupied and indifferent to the news of Mary's passing almost as if she hadn't known her, but she was unaware of Mr Henry's interference in Susan's life. She thought her apathy was because she couldn't remember meeting at the Red Spiky George exhibition.

"You probably don't remember me. We met at ..." She had no need to continue.

"Yes, I do know who you are and we met at your photography exhibition. But I really don't know when or how I got to know of Mary O'Donnell. It was a long way back." There was the murmur of resignation from Susan's end of the telephone before she spoke again. This time with a more sombre tone to her voice.

"Look, I know Mary took you in and seemed quite the saint to you, perhaps she was by then, but she wasn't always that way. I remember making a comment to you the night we bumped into one another about Marcus Allenby. Marcus was the king at Goldman Sachs and to start with, Mary was his protégée. There was so much insider trading going on in most investment banks that inquiries were springing up all over the place, but Marcus walked away from Goldman before that happened. He and Mary made millions through what they knew before anyone else did. However, they never kept it just for themselves. According to the social circles I move in you are shacked up with Sir Giles Milton QC. Ask him about Mary and Marcus. He knew them both and I heard that he didn't do too badly from the advice Marcus gave him. I'm genuinely sorry for your loss, Alicia, and I hope life pans out for you in a good way. Mine's going through a bad patch at this time, that's why I was grumpy when you rang. I hold Mary O'Donnell partially responsible for Allenby's demise. If it wasn't for her love of money then I believe his ambitions would not have reached beyond his capabilities and he'd still have a respected name on the Stock Exchange floor."

"It seems to me that you did more than enough to damage his reputation. You ran a severely vitriolic campaign in your paper denouncing him for some private sex thing he was wrapped up in. How dare you blame a dead person." There was a pause before Susan answered.

"I'm sorry. You're right. I should not have made that accusation. This is no excuse but my day is as shitty as yours." A longer pause. "No, I should never have said that either. I have no excuse. We should meet up and get to know one another better. I'm genuinely sorry. The phone is not right for this. I have to be in town tomorrow morning at eleven-thirty. I'll be no more than thirty minutes at the most. Could we do lunch do you think? Say twelve-thirty, just in case I'm running late. At the Wolseley in Piccadilly; on me? It would be my way of saying how sorry I am. Do you know the place?"

* * *

Giles opened the letter as soon as Alice arrived at his home. He noticed that she had not brought any more belongings. When asked why that was, she said she wanted to hear the contents of the letter before deciding what to do. It didn't take long. Everything Mary owned was now my sister's.

"You're now the owner of the house at Charterhouse Square with its entire contents, along with a property in Southern Ireland, in a place called Salthill, just outside Galway. She has bequeathed all her bank accounts to you. There are quite a few listed here." He began to count. "Seven in total. Three are in Switzerland." He smiled sweetly before lowering his head to read again. "A copy of this will is at her solicitors. You, or I'll do it on your behalf, must call them first thing tomorrow and make an appointment. Mary was indeed a wonderful friend to you in life, and has certainly looked after you in her tragic death."

"Was she also once a friend of yours, Giles?" Alice asked with a reservoir filled with sorrow in her eyes.

"She was, yes, but that was a long time ago, Alicia, and before I knew you."

"Why have you never told me you knew her? You've had more opportunities than we have had meals together. You could have said something as far back as when you first came to number 54? I bet you called there often enough for Mary. You could have said this morning when the hospital called, but you haven't said a word about you and her. I'm imagining that you have all kinds of things you want to hide. How about Marcus Allenby? You never said you'd met him. Why not, Giles? Is there something you would like buried about them both?" She was pacing around the front lounge of Giles's home, half angry, half bemused and in her mind; completely alone. Wanting to cry for Mary and wanting to cry for herself.

"There's nothing to hide about either of them. I have had business dealings with Marcus and personal dealings with Mary. I wasn't going to tell you because what benefit would it do you to know? Marcus introduced us when I kept my investment portfolio at Goldman's. When Allenby left to establish his venture capital company, I left my portfolio with Mary at Goldman's. Overall I thought Marcus to be a shrewd financial adviser, but he started to become too adventurous for my liking. Some of his recommendations were risky to say the least. Mary and I finished seeing each other months before she came across you. When we started dating there was no one else in my life, Alicia. The only contact I had with Mary was over investments; nothing else."

"And did those investments push you higher up Marcus Allenby's mailing list for getting news of share trading before it went public? What about invites to his kinky sex parties? Did you get any of those?"

"Did all this come from your call to Susan Rawlinson? What's she been telling you?"

"Nothing, Giles! Other than she said that you knew Mary and Marcus. Marcus for crooked share dealing that Mary knew of. It left me feeling like the odd one out. Do you know Susan?"

"I came across her ex-husband's son, Rupert Barrett, when advising a long-standing client of mine a short time ago. I distrust the press, that's why I cautioned you against getting in touch with her."

"That wasn't what I asked, Giles, was it? I asked if you knew her?"

"Whatever happened in my past is precisely that; the past. We love each other Alicia, and that is the only thing of importance.

"I'm meeting her tomorrow for lunch. I'll let you know what I think is important after that." The miserable addition of disloyalty had temporarily diluted the sadness she felt about Mary.

The two lovers sat apart from each other, abandoning words and glances, but not daring to completely ignore the present.

"Are you not moving in, Alicia?" Giles asked, faintly smiling.

"I have a lot to do at 54 and I want to keep the place exactly as it is for now. I may own the house but it was Mary's for many years and I'm not about to abandon it. I'll spend some time there and decide what to do later."

"That's very noble and perfectly understandable, but there will come a time when you will have to put the past to rest." Giles rose from where he sat and started to make his way towards the hallway. He stopped at the door, turning to address my sister.

"I'm at Southwark Crown Court in the morning. I can pick you up and take you to Mary's solicitors on my way if you wish. I know one of the partners in the firm. I'll give them a ring before I leave here. He can smooth the edges out of the probate application. He can also get you Mary's phone so you'll be able to check if you've missed telling anyone."

"I think I've managed to contact them all, but the phone would be useful." Her voice betrayed her downheartedness.

"Did you know about Mary's property near Galway, Alicia?" Giles was trying to keep her spirits up.

"I didn't, Giles. She had mentioned her childhood in Ireland and that her parents emigrated to America from there but never her house, no. I find that strange. Something I'll try to look into whilst I'm fiddling around at 54."

"I never knew she went to America. When did she return?" he asked.

"I think she must have been about eighteen or so, but again I'm not positive. There was a boy she thought she loved when her parents took her off to America. I wonder if he came from Galway?"

* * *

It was just as Mr Henry had said. I was challenged by a private security guard who pulled up in a little blue van a couple of minutes after I had passed the barrier to Hyde Park Gardens. I ignored him, only for the police to arrive a short time later, but not before I'd seen Tomlinson and he'd seen me. I'm unsure if he would have recognised me without having Marcus Allenby as close company, as it was Allenby who shouted across the road just as PC Plod was reading the riot act to me.

"Move on or I'll arrest you for causing a disturbance. And don't give me all the bollocks about human rights. You ain't gone none here, mate. Give me and my colleague one excuse to draw our sticks, chummy, and you'll make our day." Just as I was about to laugh at the thought of him and his female police colleague pulling their truncheons out in an attempt to move me, Marcus called out.

"If they don't worry you, then worry about me."

If his eyes were guns then the two bullets he fired would have done the job earlier than it actually happened, but they weren't of course and he didn't worry me either. But today was not the day to make that point. I had been told not to make a mess of anyone so I didn't. I scowled at the two police officers and stuck one finger up at the murderous looking Allenby.

"Nice place you have here, Mr Tomlinson. I'm surprised your neighbours let such a prat as Allenby come round. It's been an education. No chance of a take-away cup of tea, I suppose?"

"Come on, move," PC Plod ordered and obediently I moved on.

When I returned to Dean Street and told Mr Henry that Allenby was with Tomlinson, the beaming smile from his pearly white teeth was more than adequate to light the dimly lit office and the corridor beyond.

"Well, I think I'll go down the bookies and put a grand on a horse. Must be my lucky day. That was a bonus I never expected, Bobby. Did you see Allenby enter Tomlinson's house?"

"I didn't, boss, but I saw both of them beside the front door with the keys in Tomlinson's hand. Allenby had hold of Tomlinson's arm. When I saw that I thought Tomlinson was drunk, but he wasn't. I was shunted off before the door was opened, boss. Both of them were watching me with Marcus looking like he wanted to tear me in half. The police saw it all, as well as Tomlinson's neighbours."

"Are you sure he was angry with you and not Tomlinson?"

"Me, boss. I guess Susan, the newspaper editor, fingered me for the photos."

"Indeed, Bobby, she probably did. I want you to stay in the club for the rest of the day and through the night. Make yourself seen by plenty of people. When you leave here in the morning go straight to Hertford Street with at least one of the girls going with you. Make sure you are in company of a girl all the time. By that, Bobby, I mean do something with one that keeps you awake all night, even if it's playing tiddlywinks. It's important. I've an idea you'll be needing an alibi by morning. Do you understand me?"

"I do, Mr Henry, but can I ask why?"

"You can but if I tell you then I will probably have to kill you, Bobby. You already know too much. Just do as I say, then when the police pull you in you'll know nothing, won't you?"

"I will, boss, I mean I won't; I think."

Part Twelve

I was sitting at the counter in the bar of the Mayfair Hotel, some twelve yards away from the entrance, when Susan arrived to meet Mr Henry the following day. From where I was sitting I could smell her lemony perfume as she walked in. I had some aftershave that smelled of lemons that I would use after a heavy night of drinking to mask the smell of alcohol oozing from my skin. I wondered if that was the reason she was wearing it. Mr Henry had told me to sit where I was, but I was conscious of the annoyance I was causing the bar manager because my bulk was obstructing the narrow walk through. Susan had to push past me, that's when I could smell the booze.

"Why's he here?" Susan asked Mr Henry as she sat at his table.

"No reason other than he's my driver, Miss Rawlinson," he said as he rose to greet her. "I don't drive nowadays and it was too hot to walk."

"Would you like something to eat or will coffee suffice?" he asked as he finished his own cup.

"Tea would be better and a bottle of still water would not go amiss."

She had her back to me and there was no ignoring the beads of perspiration on her suntanned skin as they rolled down beneath the edging of her lined blouse. *Yes*, I thought, *she's been on the sauce all night.*

"Now Tomlinson's dead how does this so-called information you have impact on his memory?" she asked. "If you were after humiliating him in some way, doesn't his overnight suicide make that less interesting?" She opened the water, drinking voraciously from it without using a glass.

"How do you know it was suicide, Susan? It's my understanding that your friend Marcus Allenby is in the frame for murder. He was the last one to see Tomlinson alive and his housekeeper overheard them arguing for some time. I was reliably told that said housekeeper was in his room on the top floor when the argument was taking place. Must have been quite a loud disagreement for him to hear it high up in the roof rafters, don't you think?"

"The man sitting behind me fits the description my reporter gave of another man taken in for questioning at Paddington Police Station this morning. Care to comment, Mr Harry Henry?" Henry grinned, rocking his head to and fro in a contemptuous way before he answered.

"My driver was released after answering half a dozen or so questions, whereas Mr Allenby is still locked in a cell, Susan. He's been in custody since Tomlinson's body was found at six-thirty this morning. There really is no comparison between the two as you well know. Shall we move on to the life of Allan Henry?"

"Who?" she asked, finishing her water and ordering another.

"Phillip Barrett's lover when alive and going by his falsified name of Allan Tomlinson. Earlier today Barrett told me that my son Allan had been threatened by Marcus Allenby over Patsy Tomlinson's money. He was on his way to inform the police when he called me. Terrible thing is money. Leads men to do horrendous things. You see Tomlinson was not his real surname." From the brown leather briefcase that lay beside him, Henry withdrew a copy of the same DNA report he'd given to Allan Tomlinson the day before. He gently put it on the table in front of Susan.

"He was my son, Miss Rawlinson. Not a Tomlinson at all, this document proves it. For obvious reasons he wouldn't like to be known as the son of Soho gangster Harry Henry. You can check with the laboratory that ran the test instigated by Mr Douglas Tomlinson, who mysteriously disappeared three days after that report. All the numbers and references on the top are quite kosher. Feel free to print it as I said it, Susan; 'Soho gangster' adds a touch of romanticism. Here—" more documents were removed, "—are verifiable statements from a named local official detailing the visits my son made to care homes for vulnerable boys from 1996 to 2012. Sixteen years he was allowed to abuse children because of the influence the Tomlinson money paid for. Recently that power was instrumental in removing me from the ownership of my club, the Kiss. Your ex-husband's son, Rupert Barrett, now has his name on a document that says he owns it." He sipped his coffee before continuing.

"I don't give a rat's arse what a piece of paper says, all the same, what I do care about is that he never comes near my club and he pays me for the disturbance he's caused and the disrespect he has inflicted on me. As I told you, I'm not a greedy man, Susan and I don't really know this Rupert character. I want a token payment. Call it a gesture of goodwill. I know you and him are lovers and you know I have that photograph of your tattooed bum. It's here in my briefcase." He rummaged around until he found it. "Rather lewd I thought," he said, screwing his face up in disgust, "but who am I to judge. I have copies of course if you want to take this one home and mount it on the wall." He ordered another coffee and another water for his guest.

"Get another lemonade yourself, Bobby, put on my bill," he shouted, catching the attention of the waiter as he turned to go.

"How much would this token gesture be?" Susan asked.

"A yearly premium of fifty thousand pounds, payable tomorrow on August 16. You see I'm not out to skin people for money. All I want is recognition for the dishonour young Rupert and his cronies brought to my door. And I want them to remember it. I want the money in cash in my hands at a destination yet to be decided upon by me. I'll call you tomorrow morning around seven. By the way, it comes with the proviso that if dear Rupert is ever asked by the authorities why he takes no money from a business registered in his name, he will say that Allan Tomlinson put together a consortium of which he was the symbolic head. He was paid a one-off fee of fifty thousand pounds for his name to be used.

"I had a lengthy email from my son last night in which he not only confirmed Allenby's threats, but also how he was used by both the Barretts who forced him to finance the deal for my club. He was probably just reaching out to me in his darkest moment and cleansing his soul, the poor chap. In that email he detailed some of the intimidating remarks they made. Fifty thousand pounds, he said is what Rupert told him he had to pay as 'bunce' money. That amount should have been transferred from Allan Tomlinson's, stroke Henry's, bank account last night just before my poor son kicked the bucket."

"So, you stage-managed the suicide?" Incredulously Susan asked rather loudly.

"It's at this point in time you're going to use the Ladies on the first floor. The lift is to the right as you exit the doors from here. Bobby is going to accompany you and pat you down for any recording device you may have concealed on your person. He's thorough, but not intrusive. Do not refuse or resist, because one way or another it will be done. Leave your handbag with me, Susan. I'll have a shufti inside whilst you're gone and I'll put this photo of your bum in there while I'm about it. People might get the wrong idea if I leave it on the table bottoms up," he suppressed a laugh.

Without saying a word she made her way towards the foyer of the hotel and the lifts. I tagged behind. Once inside the toilets she offered herself without hesitation. She unbuttoned her blouse and from under her bra produced a tiny microphone connected to a small tape recorder wedged in the waistband of her briefs.
"Thank you, but I will look further."
"There is no need. That's the only one."

Taking no notice, I lifted her dress and twice turned her around; her legs were bare and she was wearing skimpy briefs, her shoes were low, backless sandals. She excited me. I removed her blouse and pulled both cups of her bra forward to look for other devices. I ran my fingers through her hair and couldn't hold myself back from lightly running my forefinger down the damp line of her spine. There was no other machine on her body.
"Now, if you will excuse me I'd like to take a pee; alone."

When we returned to the bar Mr Henry remained seated, ushering me to sit beside Susan. I handed him what I'd found. As his eyes widened he began to smile.

"I really did think that you would disappoint me, Susan. I'm sorry to say that my scepticism still holds true."

"She showed me this one, boss, without being asked."

"That was very kind of her, but it might have been because she had no choice. Susan's mobile phone was recording our conversation word by word. Did you take me for a mug?" his anger filled eyes demanded of her.

"Go do what I asked you to do, Bobby, then make your way back here." With white tightly screwed up lips and bared teeth, Mr Henry glared at her as I departed.

"There's an old saying where I came from, Miss Rawlinson; you might be able to poke an umbrella up my arse but if you think of opening it up then you'll have a lot of trouble coming your way." He delivered that remark when he changed seats and sat beside Susan.

"You do anything like this again and I will personally stuff a hot poker up your bum and burn that tattoo off at the same time, girlie. The price for keeping your perverted photo out of the press has now risen to a hundred grand. It makes me feel as though I want to wash my mouth out every time I mention it. I am holding your boyfriend responsible for this disrespect as well as you. If you, or the Barrett boy cross me I will strip the skin off your faces in such a sadistic way you'll beg me to kill you both. But let's put those thoughts of retribution to one side for a while. By this time next month I want to read how the name of Tomlinson has become a byword for all things rotten in life. I want to hear people walking up and down Dean Street saying - I've had a Tomlinson of a day, or what an effing Tomlinson day I've just had. I even want it quoted in the football press— Spurs have a 'Tomlinson' for a centre-forward. Got the picture?

"Remember there's an email on my computer alleging that Phillip Barrett and his offspring extorted money from my son. There are copies that I have printed off that are lodged with my lawyer. If one was to fall into the wrong hands it could be construed that it played a critical part in my son's mind-set preceding his death. I would hate to have to bring that email to the attention of the police, Susan, as it could also implode on Marcus. As to whether or not they would want to drop you in the shit to swim alongside them is something I can only guess it. But let's get away from threats and the like. I can guarantee the release of Marcus Allenby by a single phone call that I will make if you do as I've asked. One night banged up in Paddington nick will do him no harm. Trot off now, luv, get your boy to get the money and print that story about my late son. Say hello to Bobby if you pass him outside. He can be very cruel when I allow him to be. And don't worry, your secret is safe with me." Cruelty had a permanent home inside

Harry Henry, now glaring its face into the back of Susan Rawlinson as she was ushered away.

We didn't exactly pass each other in the way Mr Henry meant, but we did see each other again. As she opened the rear door of the white Transit van that was parked opposite where she and Mr Henry had been speaking, I was aiming the final hammer blow into the directional recording machinery in the back. I had destroyed everything there was, but as I held the door open for her and smiled, for some reason neither she nor the man lying on the floor returned that smile.

* * *

Alice was awake until the early hours of Monday morning going through more of Mary's private correspondence. It kept her busy and away from the loneliness she felt. Giles had visited but hadn't stayed for more than an hour. The cloud of embarrassment they both were under was eased away somewhat by the exchanged conciliatory words, expressing regret for some of the earlier remarks. He wasn't there when she found the letters. They were amongst memorabilia of old holidays Mary had taken on her own to Venice: a couple of water bus tickets and a museum entrance receipt. A copy of a hotel booking in Durban, South Africa and another booking made with British Airways to Athens. Perhaps, Alice thought, they were the only holidays Mary had taken because of her passion for work. Both envelopes were innocuous. The first, a frayed oblong, plain white one with the letter poking out of a corner.

Valley End
Salthill
Galway

Dearest Mary,
Only you know what is right for you. You paint this girl Alicia in a golden light as though she's an angel sent from Heaven to become whatever it is you say is missing from your life, but although God works in mysterious ways His wonders to perform I doubt if it was He that did this. More likely it was a coincidence that you met her. Whatever you decide is fine by me, my dearest, you know that, but Mary, do not let your heart rule your head in this matter. Can't you remain friends with this girl without giving her so much? Must she come to live with you? Please send me a photo of Alicia and anything else you have. I would like that very much.

Nothing has been happening here. We had enough rain in the winter to last a lifetime, but I don't expect that's the end of it. I've been up the hill to your place a few times to check on everything and all's well there. When are you coming over, Mary? I've missed you.
Loads of love,
Paula

The second letter was tucked behind two photographs; one of a white painted, cement rendered single-storey cottage with a peat-covered roof, on which the sun beamed down as it stood on the brow of a hill overlooking an angry sea in the background and a windswept emerald meadow to the front and the sides. The other, which was well thumbed and dog-eared, was of an elderly lady with long windswept red hair and a smile as wide as the deserted bay in front of which she stood. The sea was calm and the sand was a shimmering white. The cliffs were cleaved from relentless crashing Atlantic waves, greyish brown in colour, hostile yet majestic. The postmark attested to them being Irish. The same address was at the beginning of this second letter and the same signature at the end, but the dates of the postmarks were separated by more than five years. This last one being posted just eight days ago.

Dearest Mary,

You have always had a huge heart and I understand how you have felt about Alicia through the years you have known her. You are, as always, perfectly right. Who else is there deserving to share in what you have worked so hard to achieve? She has a whole wonderful life in front of her with your help and guidance behind her. I do realise what happiness her friendship has given you, it shines from every word you write. I've seen it so many times in your letters over the years and I sincerely hope that one day I'll be able to meet her. She does seem to fit the bill of being an earthly angel after all.

But why are you are speaking of your will and what will happened when you pass away? You have a glittering career and I wouldn't be out of place to add that you must have a sizeable fortune on which to retire. What will you do and where will you live when that day comes? I hope it's here, in Ireland and I hope it's soon.

I have no real news. All is well in the Fitzgerald family with no deductions or additions and the summer has been wonderful with your garden never looking better.

Why not bring Alicia over for a holiday? I know you need one and although Alicia can't work as hard as you do, a break away from London would do the both of you the world of good.

I shall spend sometime next week at Hilltop giving the place an airing just in case you can come and stay. Try and fit it in for a weekend at least, Mary.

Buckets of love,
Paula

What made you think you were dying?

Alice cried without really appreciating why. Who was the Paula with buckets filled with love and why had Mary never spoken of her? More questions, less answers. No answer to the remorse she felt for not knowing the composition of Mary, not feeling the solidity, nothing weighty to touch.

Did I honestly know you, Mary?

I allowed my imagination to go beyond what was on the surface with Spiky George, picturing another woman inside of her and the life she might have lived. Yet with you I never looked at the whole picture. Am I so shallow as to be guilty of measuring only your belongings and not the distinction that was you?

* * *

She left 54 Charterhouse Square at around ten that Monday morning, travelling with loneliness in her pocket for the short distance to the firm of solicitors that Mary had used in Goswell Road. She took all the documents that Giles had advised and was seen by Mr Isaac Brenchley the senior partner; the friend Giles had mentioned. By eleven-forty all the relevant papers regarding probate had been filled in, but there was one surprise that neither Giles nor Alice had anticipated. Mary had left instructions as to her last resting place. She wanted her ashes scattered into the wind blowing towards the sea from the bay behind her house called Hilltop at Salthill, in Ireland.

* * *

"I have just met two of the most obnoxious men I'm ever likely to meet; I hope!" Susan declared on seeing Alice seated in the coffee lounge at The Wolseley. The restaurant was busy that Monday lunchtime with the clamour of conversation and the aroma of savoury, comforting food drifting into the lounge, but the aromatic atmosphere passed Susan's attention without comment.

"Have they a table for us, Alicia?" she inquired. "Good to see you again by the way, and I'm so sorry for how rude I was."

Alice went to stand to meet her host but was beaten by Susan's bending face feigning a kiss on my sister's cheeks. As she pulled a chair away opposite from where Alice was seated, the maître d' told of a table ready for the pair in the restaurant. Susan ordered a glass of wine when shown to the table. It was then that she elaborated on her opening statement.

"One of them, a Harry Henry, owned, or still owns, an exclusive 'you know what' kind of club in Soho. Complicated situation, apparently. Your Giles is his special legal advisor and by the look of this Henry, in constant need. The other one is big and nasty. Not the sort to get on the wrong side of. Bit of a mystery, that one. Henry called him Bobby, as did a copper at Paddington Police Station this morning when he was released from being questioned about Tomlinson's death; said, 'see you another time, Bobby Brown', so I'm sure he's a regular in police stations. The police have been holding Marcus in custody for over six hours on suspicion of murder, you know."

"Really! Wow! I didn't know this Tomlinson chap. What happened?"

"You did know him, but you've forgotten. You took the photographs at his sister's wedding to Marcus Allenby. He was there. He gave her away at the ceremony. He's dead. It was a suicide," She looked carefully around then leant across the table to get closer to Alice.

"That Henry man somehow fixed it to happen. I know, sounds stupid, doesn't it! That's unless you know this Harry Henry. Anyway you haven't missed anything by not knowing Allan Tomlinson, although that wasn't his name. He was, according to Henry, his son! Creep of a person. Tomlinson and my ex had a thing going on. That's how I knew him." Susan's gaze fell on the menu as she tried hard not to look unsettled.

"So it wasn't a suicide?" Alice asked, confused, ignoring the remark about two men having a *thing* together. Susan forgot the menu for a moment.

"From what I've found out from that Henry guy, it was suicide. But there is evidence that Marcus and Tomlinson were arguing before he was found dead, along with a statement from my ex, of all people, saying that yesterday Marcus threatened to kill Tomlinson. He hasn't been arrested, just helping with enquiries, as we in the press say." She managed a strained laugh and a smile of sorts.

"Can't you tell the police what this Henry told you, Susan?"

"As I said, it's complicated, Alicia. He's a very devious character that man, and the case against Marcus doesn't stop there. Marcus lost access to any of Patsy Tomlinson's money when she died. It all went to her older brother Allan, and that's why Marcus threatened him. On the plus side of the matter, this Henry guy says all he has to do is phone the police and Marcus will be released."

"How do you know this Harry Henry chap owned or owns a club in Soho? Are you a member?" Alice asked, attempting to make sense of what she was being told.

"I'm certainly not a member," Susan replied, stony-faced. Then noticing the smile plastered across Alice's face added, "After lunch we'll go and find Rupert, who apparently owns it, but Henry contradicts that. Anyway, Giles should know the answer to that one. I think he handles all this Henry's legal affairs."

"You seem to know a lot about Giles, Susan. How's that?"

Susan's laugh was scornful. "If you're thinking he and I had a love affair then you're wrong, Alicia. Mary introduced us, when and where I honestly don't remember, but it was a long time ago and I wasn't interested in the slightest."

"I understand you're - what's the word I'm looking for? Perhaps, hitched, or an item, or just plain living with Phillip's son Rupert nowadays, Susan. How's that working for the two of you?"

"Sir Giles again, eh! Seems to be everywhere, doesn't he. It's working out really well for me, thank you. At my age it's a pleasure to have a young, fit lover. I expect Giles feels the same about you." Susan smiled in a cavalier fashion, which amused Alice who laughed softly.

"Yes, I certainly hope he does. You've had an interesting life by all accounts, Susan."

"As long as it's been sufficiently interesting for people to buy this second book I've written, then that will do. It's with the editors now and my publishers are hoping to get it out for the Christmas market."

"If you haven't a cover for it I would be happy to do the photography for you."

"Are you psychic? I'd love you to do the cover. To be honest I was going to ask you, but I didn't know how we stood as acquaintances. To be clinical I thought I'd ruined any chances I had after our telephone conversation. I didn't know if you liked me before and I was certain you didn't after it. That was really why I asked you to do lunch with me. I was nasty and knew it."

"It's not a question of like or dislike, it's simply a business proposition and I need to keep busy to keep my mind off Mary's death. I would want a percentage of the sales which, because of your, shall we say, celebrity status, I'm positive there will be plenty to go round. But I'll leave that to my agent to discuss with yours. More to the point is that I'm due to meet your Rupert in the near future and I wanted to run that past you."

"Why on earth would you need to seek my approval? He's his own man. I don't have him under lock and key. Are you going to kidnap him and sell him into the white slave trade, because if you are you have my blessing for half of the sale proceeds. I'll write you up a résumé," playfully she replied.

"No, I didn't have that in mind. It's just that Giles intimated that your relationship with Rupert was, as he put it - volatile, and I didn't want to do anything that affected it." Susan went to speak but Alice stopped her.

"Hang on, before you say anything let me just say that I think you were being less than honest when I mentioned Giles. I don't believe that the two of you never had an affair. I think you'd agree that women know these things, particularly if the man in their life is insecure when speaking of old flames. I hold no grudge against either of you over that. The past is the past. But Rupert has won a business award for being the entrepreneur for the month of July. He's being featured in *Men's Money* magazine next month and I've been commissioned to do the photography. I didn't want you thinking I was going to seduce Rupert into my bed as a way of getting back at you over Giles."

"My, my! What a strange animal you are and what an old woman Giles is. Yes! Okay we had a fling, but no more than that. It certainly was no love affair. Probably lasted three or four weeks, maybe less. And it was over three or four years ago. Well before anyone had heard of Alicia Collinson," she waited as the meal order was taken.

"Listen, Alicia, you're going through one of the worse periods in anyone's life. You've lost a person that you loved and I would think loved you. You don't need a witch like me telling you, yes, I had a thing going with the man you're now in love with. What good does that do? There is nothing in my past to worry you. I broke it off with Giles because I got bored with him. I'm like that with men in general and especially with men like him. No offence intended, Alicia. I certainly don't want to offend you, but I found him unimaginative when it came to sex. Same old, same old with him, no variety, no spice. I had better add, in those days, hadn't I? And it was a long time ago." An indefinable smile spread across her face, somewhere between competitive and reassuring.

"Volatile, he said, did he? I'm surprised he knows what being volatile means. Perhaps you have excited his sexual drive so much that he can conjure up words like volatile. I honestly have no idea why he would want to speak of me. As I said, Rupert is his own man. I'm not surprised he's won an award as he never stops working. Most of his money is in nightclubs but not here in London, in and around Manchester and Liverpool. He has a very large house and grounds in Cheshire where he spends most of his time. Originally I came from more or less the same area so we have that in common, along with Phillip of course being both our mistake and misfortune. Have him, Alicia. Use him for your photos and for any vigour that may be missing in your enamoured connection with the law. He and I are very discreet when it comes to those we have an intimacy towards." The licentiousness of Susan's scrutinising look was not missed by Alice.

"We have a common ability, you and I, Susan, one where we embellish the mundane. You with your command of the English language. Daily turning a drab news report into a multi-dimensional story of intrigue and plot to capture the imagination of those who can't live without your conjecture, and me turning an ordinary face or scene into something more alluring and mysterious." Susan was quick in reply.

"But with your work you cannot turn an ugly picture into something it's not, whereas that's where I'm expected to excel. If I don't, and sales figures fall, then the newspaper's owners call me up and sack me over the phone. If you fail you just sell less and lose your reputation."

"I'd go broke and so would you, Susan."

"Not me, dear. I'd move on."

"Which reminds me; I'm off to Ireland near the end of this week to follow Mary's last wish regarding her ashes. Rupert's photograph needs to be on the cover of the September edition of *Men's Money*. I will need him quite soon. Perhaps he can ring me when I'm away and we can fix a date."

"Is Giles going with you to Ireland?" Susan asked with a wink.

"No, he's all yours," Alice responded with a laughing smile.

"You'll have more fun scattering ashes than I would if I took you up on your offer."

Part Thirteen

The air was soft and fragrant after the touch of summer rain as Alice travelled the short journey from Galway, alighting from a cab outside what was once Mary's home above a secluded cove at Salthill. Despite the fact that she had tried hard not to think of how Mary's cottage would look, it had been impossible, but what greeted her was far from her expectations. She had imagined it would be similar if not the same as the one in the photograph she'd found in Mary's desk; a white painted, cement rendered quaint cottage with a peat-covered roof and perhaps a wisp of smoke rising from its single chimney carrying the sweet smell of baking bread on the wind, but although it was painted white that's where any similarity ended. It was huge. Three floors of wide, tall balconied windows and, on the ground floor, an ornate veranda disappearing from the front of the house around each side towards the rear. Grey slates had replaced the peat on the roof where there was no sign of aromatic smoke from any chimney. A garage for least two cars stood on the western edge with a hard drive joining it to the road. From Galway the lanes had been bordered by rolling hills of verdant grass with viridescent vegetation, but the garden that spilled from the O'Donnell home onto the roadway was a chaotic kaleidoscope of colourful wild flowers, roses and honeysuckle dancing together.

As Alice was about to pay the taxi driver, who stood patiently with her small suitcase in one hand and a cigarette in the other, one of the double frontal doors to the house opened and a short portly woman with long curly, unruly red hair stood there, her hands on both hips laughing gleefully. Above her head, fixed to building, was the sign saying, Hilltop.

"I hope you're about to charge the young lady the correct amount, Connor, 'cos if you're not I'll be telling your Ma next time I see her and she won't be best pleased. The lady in front of you was Mary O'Donnell's best friend and now she's the new mistress of the house. So you'll be having a care to your arithmetic now, won't you."

"Paula?" Alice excitedly asked as driver Connor stood to attention, discarding his cigarette and stamping on it as if the clock had been turned back to when he was one of Paula's students at the primary school where she had been the headmistress.

"And aren't you the very vision of beauty I imagined you to be, Alicia Collinson," she announced as she twisted her way through the gently swaying patterns of disorganised charm towards the road. "You are exactly as dear Mary described you. Welcome to the cnoc, as we call a hill in these parts."

Paula was seventy-eight years of age with two hundred years of laughter etched around eyes as blue as the sea that sparkled in the sunlight and a voice like a gentle wave lapping at the cliffs beyond.

"Mary's parents originally lived here, you know," she stated as she took hold of both Alice's arms. "I grew up with them. I saw them go to America and I was here to welcome them back. If you're wondering if you have an old woman as a lodger then let me put your mind to rest. I live down the road a piece, at a house called Valley End. You would have passed by my little home in Connor's taxi. It's nothing as grand as this one."

The two women stopped staring at each other and turned to face the imposing building.

"This place was always full of merriment and fun even when both Daniel and Aileene passed over. We have enough rain in these parts to water the flowers and the carpets inside won't welcome any tears, my girl. Come, I've prepared a light lunch to welcome you to Ireland. *Céad Mile Fáilte*. It means welcome, and that's the last bit of Irish you'll be hearing from me, Alicia." With that Paula, carrying my sister's case, made off towards the rear of the house by way of a well-trodden, grassy path along the side.

"A nephew of mine owns a very large gardening business. I think he employs the whole family in it," she said with a huge smile covering her face.

"His company has contracts with all the town councils in the county boroughs of Waterford, Limerick as well as here in Galway. It's a huge concern. I'm very proud of him. Once in a while," Paula winked at Alice, "He sends someone up here to keep the gardens from misbehaving when God is the only one caring for it. The back garden is where his men do the most work and the sitting, I'm guessing."

"Was he the mysterious man Mary loved who never loved her back?"

"Oh, you know of him, do you? He loved her all right. Did when she left and still did when she came home. I would be surprised if he has changed much in that regard down the years." There was a brief pause to Paula's account whilst Alice stared open-mouthed at her.

"As no doubt we will become more acquainted with each other than we are now, I may as well shatter any illusions you have of me sooner than later." Her laughter lines were overshadowed by a dour expression.

"It was my doing that Mary and my nephew parted. His name is Liam Fitzgerald, by the way. If you stay any length of time he'll be around, in fact we will probably be getting a few new faces finding their way up the hill after Connor tells them of a pretty girl moving in at Hilltop."

"You've left a huge gap in that explanation, Paula. What did you do to stop Mary and Liam seeing each other?" Alice asked with a look of thorough astonishment on her face.

The pair stopped in a little dip in the path where the sun was shining directly behind Paula, making her silhouette seem spiritual and saintly.

"To fully answer that question, Alicia, you must understand the times then and us queer folk in this part of Ireland. Galway may seem quite a large town to you but it's not, and back in those days it was even smaller. Opportunities for employment are still few and far between. The families that live in these parts can, in the main, count back centuries of forefathers from the same house that they now live in. There are records going back to 1459 mentioning my family coming from these parts in this Emerald Isle. I'm the matriarchal head of this one and have been for a considerable time. I have never married, but I had four sister who did, and two brothers who did. I had enough to worry about with all them and the others in this close tribe called the Fitzgeralds. The O'Donnells had a shorter connection. Nevertheless, they belonged here. I told Liam that Mary was destined for a life beyond these shores and if he proposed marriage she would accept, making him a happy man but eventually making her a resentful prisoner. It wouldn't work, I told him, and he told Mary that he didn't love her when really he did. That's the long and short of it." She turned to go, but hadn't quite finished.

"I bet you're thinking I'm a wicked woman who should have kept her nose out of their business?"

"I'm not made that way, Paula. I've made too many mistakes in my short life to be the judge of others' lives. That said, I am thinking you have a lot of power over members of your family. As you rightly implied, we don't know each other. Nevertheless, I know enough to realise you said it to protect Mary."

"That I did, and I was right," Paula replied.

"How did she take Liam's rejection?"

"To be honest with you, I can't remember too well. It was a long time ago, Alicia. But Mary was an unemotional girl all her life. She was the cool-headed one was Mary. I can't ever remember her being flustered or in a state about something."

'*Really,* Alice thought. *Not even for being raped?*'

"Did you notice if she had changed much when she returned from America?" Nibbling at the edges of the question Alice wanted to ask but didn't know how.

"Yes, in some ways she had. I thought for a while she was less assured of herself, but if she was, her confidence wasn't missing for long. Adolescence plays tricks in young people's minds."

"Hmm, you're probably right." Unsure of how to proceed, Alice gave a wide berth to Paula's omission of the rape and abortion.

"Mary left instructions in her will about the scatting of her ashes in the bay, Paula. She asked if we could do it together. Perhaps she had a favourite spot that only you would know of? Maybe later today or tomorrow we could do that, as I can only stay for a few days on this trip."

"Yes, Mary told me of her wishes. I'm sorry if I was a little snappy at you a few minutes ago. Her death has touched me deeply. I never thought she would go before me."

"There's no need to apologise. I'm the stranger who walked into your life, and in any case I'm on your side. If Liam and Mary had married, she and I would never have met and I would have missed out on the love of a wonderful woman." The two women hugged each other, staying in the embrace until Alice broke away.

"Did Mary tell you of her illness, Paula?" The two had reached the back door, when Alice faced the pain of not knowing Mary as well as she thought she had.

"That she did. Her death followed unkindly fast from when that happened. She telephoned me around eleven on the Friday morning saying she'd been admitted to hospital. Very calmly she added she wouldn't be coming out. The doctors had told her what was wrong and that's when she spoke of her ashes. She was very matter of fact about it. As though she was dictating a shopping list. No tears, no," she never finished that sentence.

"She never told me a thing," Alice replied, broken-hearted. "The doctor I saw said it was pancreatic cancer. I found nothing amongst Mary's belongings to indicate that she knew. The only thing I found was an envelope addressed to me with her will inside. I was devastated. I still am. The truth is I don't know the words to describe how I feel." She was on the point of ignoring Paula's instructions about not crying.

"Mary told me that she couldn't tell you, Alicia. She said she would have broken down before the words had left her mouth. She was as cool as a cucumber over it all until I mentioned your name, then I could make no sense of what she was saying through her tears. There was one thing I did clearly hear. She said it was leaving you that was the hardest to face. After that, I heard her say something strange that I still cannot figure out— *Ask Alicia to send the birthday cards for me.* But come on. Tell me about that over a cup of tea. We will both be in tears any minute now and that won't do either of us, or Mary, any good."

Paula opened the door and Alicia stepped into the house. As she turned back to face Paula she saw the view that greeted Mary everyday she spent here on the hill looking down into the bay.

"What a fairy-tale picture you had here, Mary. What made you ever want to leave?" she said aloud to her departed friend. Paula came to rescue my sister from the wave of sorrow that was going to engulf her.

"That view is why Mary's great-great-great-grandfather had the house built here. There's a funny story attached to that. Sadly a typical Irish one."

"Irish but sad? That doesn't sound quite right. I'm intrigued."

"It goes back many a year to when I think Mary's great-great-great-grandfather first arrived on this side of Ireland. He was escaping from an English court of law, so the story goes, for jilting his bride; the daughter of an English aristocrat, but you know what liars Englishmen can be, no doubt, Alicia." They smiled at each other. "Anyway, here he was on Fitzgerald land in love with a view, handsome, twenty-something and looking for a hideaway. My great-whatever-grandfather, and remember this story has been passed down many generations so it's probably a variation of the truth, offered him a hideaway, near where my house now stands, if he was to marry the youngest Fitzgerald daughter. She was, so it's been told; a little on the ugly side, the poor lass." Paula burst out laughing which Alice had no chance not to follow.

"Mary's relative, can't keep saying all those greats, agreed if my relative threw in this plot of land to build his house. My one said no, but could not leave it there. He didn't want the disgrace of having a daughter no one, not even an escaping Englishman, wanted to marry. They had a contest to settle the dispute. Can you see the rock that juts out over there?" Paula took Alice's arm and pointed to a large overhanging rock about two hundred yards beyond the bay.

"My relative proposed a race to the top of that rock, from here where we stand when the tide was at its fullest. My family were fishermen and, so I'm told, good swimmers and climbers. The stakes were simple; the Fitzgeralds would give O'Donnell a house and new identity for as long as he needed it if he married the daughter. Or, if he won the race, they would give him that new identity and give him this spot to build his house. On one condition; he would still have to marry the daughter. It would seem that O'Donnell was a better swimmer and climber who loved this spot more than he disliked the Fitzgerald girl."

"And how long ago was that, Paula?" Alice asked, laughing loudly.

"I've heard it was the mid-1800s and I've also heard it was the mid-1700s. Take your pick, Alicia."

* * *

Mr Henry chose to meet with Rupert Barrett in his office at the club. From the little mutterings he made I gathered it was to rub Barrett's nose into the fact that the Kiss was never his in the first place, and never would be. The club had yet to open when he arrived via the back stairs. I opened the door for him.

"Here's your hundred grand of dirty money, Henry," he threw a canvas bag across the floor which stopped when it hit the side of Mr Henry's desk. Mr Henry glanced down at it from where he stood.

"I was under the impression that this was a legitimate deal we had here. Somehow you and your lawyer friend untangled it and stitched me up. I don't know how you made the Tomlinson guy top himself, but if I ever get the chance of repaying you in kind then rest assured I will." He was as tall as me in stature but not so broad nor as heavily built. Brown hair and hazel eyed. I was unclear as to the colour of a real bear's eyes, but if they were hazel then yes, with some imagination, he resembled a bear.

"Now we know two facts about bears, Bobby."

"We do, Mr Henry?" I replied, wondering where this enlightenment was going.

"Aren't you listening, Bobby? Not only do bears eat honey they talk too much. And you know what people say about those who talk too much, don't you?"

"I don't think I do, Mr Henry."

"It's always the empty cans that make the most noise. That's what they say." He paused to light his first cigar of the day. "If I was going to kill someone I wouldn't tell them. That would be silly. I'd let them wait, wondering how I was going to do it. How about you, Bobby? Would you tell someone you were going to kill them before you did?"

"I certainly would not, boss. That would be plain stupid," I replied, looking into the Bear's eyes.

"And there we have it." He drew heavily on his cigar, exhaling the cloudy smoke as he spoke. "We both think you're a clown, Rupert Barrett, and better off in a circus. Don't come anywhere near me in the future. Bobby here might like it if you did. But believe me; you won't like it at all."

He left by way of the yard and then the alleyway beyond, slamming the door behind him and kicking a dustbin. But there was nothing to suggest anything worse was to follow.

Part Fourteen

It was sometime in the afternoon on the Sunday, Alice's second day at Hilltop, that Paula mentioned me. Whether it was the morning mass at Saint Ignatius or the simple fact that the rain had shuffled Paula's train of thought, who knows, but it was in the kitchen of Mary's old home that the name of Bobby Brown crept into the conversation by way of the back door, stayed lounging on a sofa during their lunch and finally took up residence by the time both Alice and Paula were a bit tipsy.

"Give me five minutes to change out of my Sunday best, Alicia, and I'll be in for some of that roast chicken of yours you're promising and a glass or two of the sparkling stuff. My nose had adjusted to the bubbles by the time I rolled down the hill last night." Her lyrical voice was in a dancing mood over the telephone which the mile long walk from the church had not blunted nor moderated from her 'soft shoe reel' of the previous evening.

Whilst Paula sat in the church pew controlling her chirpy feet, Alice had wandered along a steep, descending path from the windswept clifftop down to the sheltered cove. Mary's cove, her place to think, dream and perhaps plan the ashes-spreading ritual. Alice leant against a rock and gazed out to sea wondering if the sand beneath her feet was where Mary sat when she came here. She decided it was and began a silent conversation with her deceased friend. It ended with the screaming question of — why —joining the flood of tears that only the sea witnessed and the wind heard.

* * *

Good as her word, Paula made it in time for the piping hot Sunday roast and the first of a few glasses of the 'sparkling stuff.'

"I made a few enquiries when Mary first told me of you, but I bet that comes as no surprise. I found your real name and your twin brother at the same time."

"You found Tom? But why did you need to? And why delve into me, Paula?"

"Simple really," she replied on finishing her first glass and immediately refilling it. "I wouldn't be wanting Mary taken for a ride or to befriend a liar and a crook, now would I?" She was smiling as she declared, but her next question carried implications of an all too different nature.

"Why did you change your name, Alicia?"

"I could tell you a lie and say it was to turn a plain name into something more chic and fashionable, but no, that was not the reason. I didn't want to be found by Tom or dragged back into my past by anyone. I wanted a new beginning. That might sound callous and selfish but that's what I wanted." Alice and Paula locked eyes and neither blinked before my sister began to distance herself immeasurably from me.

"At first I did it myself on any papers that name was on. I simply altered the 'e' of Alice to an 'i' then added an 'a' and wrote the 'on' to Collins. I told my foster mother my plans and she helped me to get a Post Office savings book with my new name and a bank letter addressed to Alicia Collinson sent to her address. I told her I was going and not to worry about me. I guess she must have told the authorities, but by then it didn't matter what I was called because I was sleeping rough, or in squats, where nobody bothered with an identity. Shortly after Mary took me in she got me a mobile phone. That resulted in a telephone account in my name which I used to open a proper bank account. Later, I had a virus infection and I had to find a doctor. I told them I'd lost my original medical card so I got one sent to the London address with my new name. My passport carries Collinson."

"Tom hasn't found you, so it must have worked."

"But it didn't work for you, Paula?"

"I'm going to tell you a secret that nobody knows, not even Mary, God rest her soul." She made the sign of the cross before sweeping some wayward curls away from her face with one hand and replenishing her glass with the other.

"I did some work for the British during the Troubles. It wasn't much, but it would cost me my life if anyone knew."

"Good grief, Paula! Are you sure you want to tell me? You don't know me that well." Alice stood and fetched another bottle of sparkling wine, then sat wearing a puzzled look.

"Well, I think I do, young lady. I lost a nephew and a niece to an IRA bomb in Newry, in Northern Ireland. All the Fitzgeralds are catholics, and I think I can speak for all of them and say we couldn't care less if the Protestants in the North want to stay under British rule. But I care passionately about my family. I hated the IRA from then on. I won't burden you with details of the circuitous route I had to go down to safely reach someone inside British intelligence, be that as it may, I got there and started to pass information.

"This shoreline has masses of coves which the IRA used for many things. One was to ferry their men fleeing from some atrocity or another they'd caused in the North. Once here, he or she would change their name in order to hide out in the South, or at least become less noticeable. There was a command network based in Galway run by a father and his two son. They were fisherman by trade. They would take these escaping murderers in their boat to southern parts of England on occasions, but more often than not to met bigger ships loaded with guns and the 'cargos' would be exchanged. I traced some of those in the chain and passed on all that I'd found out. I was good at what I did. I was told, unofficially I'd better add, that the SAS got a few, including the family who were in charge of it all."

"Wow! Mata Hari is alive and living near Galway. I suppose I should say thank you on behalf of the British for helping us out, but I'm guessing you would rather I say nothing by the look on your face. Plus I'm a bit young to know much of that. I take it you used what you'd learned to trace my brother and me?"

"I did, and like most things it's not difficult if you know what you're doing and where to look. It comes down to silly little things in the end and in any case you hadn't buried your past and tried to disappear." Paula smiled in a maternal way.

"I will admit that your altered name did worry me at first. Mary would have none of it though. In spite of all the dangers I pointed out to her, she stuck to her decision and would not budge. I came around to her way of thinking when I could see you going down another path than that of your brother. He went into detention centres and then more and more prisons, while you knuckled down to your studies. Mary said it was a natural thing to do; change your name, if you wanted to escape from the past."

"I bet Tom would like to forget his past. Prisons! You say there were many. Was there anything really serious he did to be put in prison?" Alice asked.

"It depends on how you define serious. He never murdered anyone if that's what you mean, but he did rob banks, carried guns and I found lots on the internet about his involvement in violence. Came close to murder on a couple of occasions, so I read." Paula replied with a stern look on her face. "Was Tom the only reason for change?" She asked reaching for her glass.

* * *

This is where I suppose I should hang my head in shame, but it's too late for my regrets. Yes, I can accept I was her reason to become a Collinson and with that thought I can undeniably understand her rationality, but my sanity tails away and refuses to acknowledge what then happened as being a fault of mine alone.

* * *

"I saw a newspaper report about him kidnapping a banker and holding his wife and kids at gunpoint. I wanted nothing to do with a life like that. He was becoming a selfish bully to everyone we knew before both our parents had died. Our surname of Collins was the link so I broke it. I'm not surprised he went the way he did. What's he doing now, Paula?"

"He's using a different name, but hasn't completely changed his way of life."

"What's the name he's using?"

"Bobby Brown, he works for a very discreditable man named Harry Henry in a sex club in London." Paula noticed the incredulous look on Alice's face. "Have you heard either of those name before, Alicia?"

"Yes! I heard both names a few days before I came to Ireland. But it wasn't said to me that Bobby Brown was my brother. The person who told me did not know that. The club's name is the Kiss I believe, and Mary knew of the club as she mentioned it to me at least once, if not more times. We both knew a man who used it; a Marcus Allenby. Did Mary ever mention him to you, Paula?"

"The name sounds familiar, yes, but the club doesn't."

"Did Mary know my brother and Bobby Brown were the same person?"

"I think I had mentioned it, but I'm not sure. It wasn't as though the two of us saw each other much, or wrote more than once a month and there were more things to talk about than just you two."

"Do you think that my twin brother knows about me? Only if he did I don't know what I'd do."

"I can't think of how he would know, Alicia. I certainly have not spoken of it to anyone and I know Mary would not have communicated with him without speaking to you first. She was well aware of how much pain he could cause."

Alice fell silent for a while and as the furrows deepened on her brow she worried about Mary's knowledge of a Bobby Brown. Did she say something about him to someone in an unguarded moment?

Can I rely completely on her discretion?

"Why wouldn't Mary tell me she'd found Tom, Paula? What on earth was she afraid of? It wasn't as though we were close and I'd run off to join him in this club you mentioned."

"If it's the truth according to Saint Paula you're after, and not from a bubbly bottle, then I believe Mary was jealous of him. I only have her letters to go by, but had I not known otherwise I would have believed you were her daughter by the way she spoke of you. On more than one occasion she wrote that she felt privileged to be in your company. She thought it was magnificent what you'd achieved. I can imagine how she wouldn't want to share you, especially to a twin brother." She took another mouthful of wine, replacing her glass on the table with a fretful frown on her face.

"Mary had been on her own for a long time. Both her parents had died before she reached twenty-one. I know her work kept her busy and perhaps too busy to socialise sometimes, but she needed to be needed and I'm not belittling you by saying that. After Aileene died I was the only one she had. Daniel had passed the year before and there was nobody other than me to tell her worries to. I hope I filled part of Aileene's shoes in being her second mum. When she told me she was to leave everything of hers to you I was lost for words. I expected to be long-gone before that was ever spoken of. Like you I was not prepared for her to die." Her voice carried her own despondency and her eyes betrayed how close to tears she was.

"I would have liked to have known more about my brother," reflectively Alice replied, contemplating a utopian past that could never have occurred. Paula composed herself, pulling back from any display of sorrow.

"You say that for all the right reasons a girl like you would think of, but your brother is a thief and a man of violence. You are a well-known name and must have well-known friends. When Mary had the time to phone me, she wouldn't stop talking about your exhibitions. Do you know, I think that's where I heard her say the name of Marcus. Didn't he buy a lot of your photographs?"

"He did buy a lot at my first exhibition, yes."

"How do you think your brother would fit into this social-circle of yours? His hands would be rubbing together in delight all day long having a rich sister with wealthy friends? The only worry he would have to deal with, is which one to rob first if it wasn't going to be you."

"I realise what you're saying, but he's my brother. What should I do?"

"We have to scatter Mary's ashes before we do another thing so that's what we'll do before these bubbles go all the way down to my feet. Then we'll have a think about this other matter. I will need your help along the path down into the bay where we can say a few words. There's a rock where she would sit on the sand for hours just thinking of what I don't know. It's a bit of climb coming back but there's a ledge halfway up. I might have to park myself there for a couple of minutes."

With the confident hand of a woman familiar with the winds around the cove of Salthill, Paula despatched Mary's ashes towards the Atlantic Ocean then both women bowed their heads in respect and wished their friend farewell. After a few minutes under the warm afternoon sun they started on the climb back up the winding path from the bay and Alice had a proposal which she put to Paula.

"As I said, I can only stay for a short while but I would love you to show me the coves around Salthill, if you're up for it, Paula. We'll hire a car and just drive where the fancy takes us. I'll take the photographs and you can tell me more stories about Mary, her family and how many races the O'Donnells and the Fitzgeralds took part in. I would love that, Paula."

"In that case we'd better be saving what's left of those sparkling wines for the journey, my girl. Can be thirsty work, can exploration."

"We'll stop at an off-licence on the way to replenish our stocks," a laughing Alice replied.

"And then we could buy some cheese and soda bread for good company and have a picnic somewhere. I'll find some cutlery to take with us. And oh yes, Mary had some plastic glasses she used for the beach. I'll find those as well."

When the returning pair reached the ledge that Paula had spoken of, she sat and from a pocket withdrew a pencil and notebook in which she listed the required utensils. It was as they set-off for the more gentle part of the climb that an innocent Paula stepped into the minefield that I had left in an earlier part of this story.

"When the O'Donnell's left for America, Aileene told me that it would be for at least five years if not ten, but before two had past they were home. Aileene never really told me why. She always seemed too busy to talk, or she would shoo me away with a tale or two. One spring day, when we were on the clifftop, minding our own business, she told me Mary had been in a road accident and as a result was now infertile. I never pushed the point. Aileene said she didn't want to talk about it and not to question Mary, so I didn't. I wonder if she had ever mentioned it to you, Alicia?" Alice came to an immediate stop.

"Infertile! What do you mean you never asked Mary or Aileene about it. You must have! It can't be everyday news around here. What were you thinking of, Paula?"

"I didn't know how to, Alicia. What was I to say; 'Hi, Mary, sorry to hear you had an accident in America that left you infertile?' When all the time I wanted to ask, did you get yourself pregnant and was it the abortion going wrong that caused your inability to ever conceive children? Did she say anything at all to you?"

My sister had no thought of confirming the rape and the abortion to Paula, who clearly didn't know, nor telling of the unsent birthday cards. Nothing was as important as Mary's infertility and why she had filled the gap of a child with my sister. The questions bounced around inside her head until all were answered except one—If she had known of Mary's infertility would that have made a difference?

"You were right not to ask Mary, or her mother, Paula. It was their business to tell you or not. It will have to remain as a mystery to us both just as my brother is to me."

She allowed Paula to pass and walked behind her with yet another reason to empty the well of tears.

What a woman you were, Mary, and now I know what you meant when you said that your money had not bought you happiness. What could? I hope and pray that when we were together you were happy, because you definitely made me happy. I also hope that in the short time we had I did become the daughter you wanted. When we were together I learned a lot from you, now I have to stand on my own two feet. The decisions to make are mine to make and there's no point in regrets. Is there!

* * *

During the month of August the Kiss Club was relatively quiet, as most of the punters took the time off to spend with their school holidaying children playing at happy families while home or abroad; even Marcus Allenby was away. The girls had more spare time on their hands than they knew what to do with and I was equally under-employed. I took a break away from the club, taking Gabriella with me. She had family living in Manchester so that's where we went. We stayed for two nights, both of which I slept on the sofa; not through choice, nor to save anyone's embarrassment. The night before we returned to London we paid a visit to Barrett's *Bear Cave* club in the city just to be nosy and the want of something to do. I had been back at the Kiss for about four days when an envelope, addressed to me, was delivered by a motorcycle courier. It contained three thousand pound in cash and a note that said, 'The cheapest funeral costs about £2000 on average. Keep the change for your piss-up.'

When I questioned the motorcyclist, he said he had come from Manchester but did not know how and when the envelope arrived at the dispatch office where he had been given it. All he knew was that he was tired from the arduous ride. The only one I could think of who would send such a provocative note would be Marcus, but he lived the other side of Hyde Park, close to me here in London and a long way from Manchester.

* * *

Rupert followed Susan's instructions to telephone Alice, calling on the day before she left for Ireland. She asked him if he knew Marcus Allenby as they had the game of rugby in common, to which he replied that Allenby was to be his guest from the Monday of the following week. Alice explained to Paula how her workload for August prevented her from staying past Wednesday, but in spite of that she hoped to come back before the month ran out. She caught the ferry from Dublin to Liverpool early Wednesday morning, then took a taxi to Rupert Barrett's home in the village of Mobberley near Knutsford in Cheshire. Marcus Allenby was there. All fitted together so conveniently and the head and shoulder shot of Rupert exiting his swimming pool that later appeared on the front cover of *Men's Money* was not the only outcome of that meeting, nor her stay at Rupert's house and return to London in the company of Marcus Allenby. There were other things of note concluded near Manchester and in Ireland.

Part Fifteen

Back At the Dinner Party

"Where's this fascination with the truth come from, Alicia? I've never heard you mention it before." It was Sir Giles who questioned her conviction.

"It's not so much the truth I'm on about, it's the lies that we all accept in our everyday lives that interest me. Perhaps the avoidance of truth is closer to it. The woman and child in Harrods was a foolish example of mine. As you rightly said, Giles, the boy will realise in time that not all oranges come from Spain. It's as I say; more the lies we tell to avoid telling the truth."

"Are you guilty of that, Alicia?" Rupert asked.

"I guess I must be as I've certainly misled some people to believe that I liked them when in truth I didn't."

"Any one of us sitting here?" Rupert replied, smiling smugly.

"I would advise you not to answer that, my dear, as you may insult both our guests," with a huge grin Giles added.

"If your memory is any good you'll remember insulting me, Giles; twice! Once when you screwed up with that first agreement we signed over the Kiss Club, and second when you never lived up to your word and reputation with Marcus Allenby. What's done is done, but you damaged your reputation with me." A brooding Bear was stretching his claws.

"That's all best forgotten, Rupert and you know it." Susan came to Giles's defence. "We have all moved on and Alicia won't know what you're talking about. As for Marcus, he was guilty. How could he not be? Look what Giles did for him when things were looking very ugly over that Tomlinson suicide. Without Giles both occasions could have been seriously worse. He could have been charged with murder then. You can't argue about being charged with carrying an offensive weapon when you have a gun tucked down your pants and you're five hundred yards from a dead body. Carrying a weapon with intent to kill would have been a different story, but Giles got him off that charge. He would have gone down for a lot longer if convicted with that."

"I do know what Rupert is talking about, Susan, as it was you who told me of Harry Henry and that Kiss Club of his. I was also in court for some of the trial." Alice confessed.

"Completely against my advice, I'll add." Giles was never one to miss an opportunity to play the wounded party.

"But what if Marcus deserved to be sent down for murder?" Alice's examining eyes alternated from one unemotional face to another, not finding an answer.

"What if you arranged the meeting Rupert, and sent Marcus to meet Bobby Brown knowing what he was going to do?"

"Wow, love you too, Alicia! Where did that spring from? Marcus's gun was not fired so how did he murder two men?" An injured Rupert replied.

"No, I didn't say Marcus murdered anyone. I only said you sent him to do it but someone got there first."

"And did I want this Harry Henry murdered too, Alicia?" Although the smug smile had not left Rupert's face, Susan was looking uncomfortable with the conversation. She glanced at Giles for support.

"I have to admit to being with Rupert on this. What's the basis for your allegations, Alicia?" Giles asked, shaking his head.

"I have the same amount of evidence that the police had after Harry Henry contacted them saying that Tomlinson committed suicide because he had discovered he was Henry's son. Henry told them of a conversation he had with Tomlinson the previous day and Allenby walked free. Like them I have no evidence. I have nothing but a heart that's been broken too many times to carry on. I've lost Mary and I've lost the brother I never knew. Bobby Brown's other name was Tom Collins. He was my twin brother."

For a lie to add piquancy to a story, the story would be factual. Fantasy is the lie that stimulates and excites. But if the factual story is contrived or fallacious then it's the fantasy that is the truth.

Part Sixteen

Back To The Story That Had No Beginning

Rupert Barrett's communication with Harry Henry was delivered in person the same day as the three thousand pound from Manchester arrived. I had not told Mr Henry of that parcel. The pair did not meet at the Kiss, they met at a disused shop premises in Berners Street, north of Oxford Street, five hundred yards from the Kiss. Outside was a 'To Let' sign.

"I'm going to rent this place, convert it and open it up as a club. Take me three months to complete. Be open for Christmas, Harry. I'll send you an invitation to the opening night." Mr Henry did not approve of such familiarity.

"You will address me as Mr Henry and I thought I made myself perfectly clear that I would not like you being in competition near me. You seemed in agreement when I mentioned my opposition to such a move. What gave you the balls to front me up?"

"Balls! Who do you think are? You know precisely why I'm doing this. Did you think I was going to roll over and allow you to waltz in to take me out? Cos I'm not! You try to touch me here or in Manchester and you'll have a war, the like of which has never been seen before. Have you got that, pal?" Mr Henry was stunned!

"Operate in Manchester? Me? Are you crazy? What the fuck for? I don't even know where it is. Why would I want to go where it's cold and wet? Bad for the bones at my time of life. Whatever gave you that idea?"

"Your tosser Bobby Brown showing up at a place of mine last Wednesday night with that tart Gabriella, that's what gave me the idea. If you hadn't sent him to size up the trade, then what was it for?"

"No! I did not authorise that. Nor do I like the sound of it. I have a suggestion, Rupert. Let's find a bar and have a chat."

* * *

"He's gone too far this time, Bobby. I want you to finish it."

"Who's gone too far, boss?"

"That Rupert the bear, Barrett, is who."

"What's he done, boss?"

"It's not what he's done it's what he's saying about you and me. He's implying that we are - I'm not repeating the gutter language he used. Can you handle him on your own or you want help in the matter?"

"Nah, I can take him, boss. How far do you want me to go with him?"

"My view on life is quite straightforward in matters such as this. Life is full of violence, corruption and far too many tosspots. I will not have him disrespecting me in what he says to people that I know." He waved his mobile phone in the air to add poignancy to his outrage.

"There are hundreds of names in this phone of mine who either fear me, need me or the occasional one or two who actually love me. I want it to stay that way. I want you to make sure I'm never disturbed by him again."

"I'll fix a meet with him. Somewhere nice and quiet. I'll get it done as soon as, boss."

"Fine! But you let me know when and where that is."

I had my own reasons to want to do away with Marcus Allenby more than Rupert Barrett, but I had no liking of Barrett so he would do. I visited a friend's house where I'd hidden a sawn-off shotgun in his greenhouse under the tomatoes. He and the tomatoes weren't that pleased, but I was.

"I'm all set for tonight, Mr Henry. I'm meeting Barrett at two in the morning in Battersea Park by the Pagoda. I've got a shooter. I told him I had some information on you that I wanted to sell."

"Are you going on your own, Bobby?"

"I am, boss. I don't believe I need anyone. Plus it keeps the witnesses down to just me."

"Are you sure you wouldn't like me to send someone with you?"

"Nah, boss, I prefer to be on my own. Have a nice quiet night."

I got to the appointed place close on an hour before Barrett was due. I holed up where I had chosen. In the shadows of a tree where I looked out onto the moonlit path with the silvery river behind. I put two cartridges in the gun and took the safety off. I never heard a footstep nor the shot that drilled through my head and lodged into the tree. I never saw my killer and I can't clearly see who it was now. But I did hear a voice!

Part Seventeen

Back At the Dinner Party

"Why didn't you say that at the time, Alicia? Why didn't you say he was your brother?" It was Susan who asked. Rupert and Giles looked vacantly at one another, until Rupert was the first who spoke.

"I don't understand why you went to all this trouble to tell us. Why go all the way around the houses talking about lies when it was your brother you wanted to speak about?"

"It would have made no difference to the outcome of the trial." It was Giles who spoke, addressing Rupert.

"What about when you went to court to watch Marcus being tried? Did you not want to say anything then?" Susan asked.

"I couldn't see how my relationship to Bobby Brown would have helped. I thought it would compromise Marcus at the trial. I didn't want to make things worse for him."

"How do you mean worse? The gun they found on him had not been fired!" Susan exclaimed. "So how could anything you say make it worse?"

"I know that and I know it was not the gun that killed Harry Henry. I heard it given in evidence that it was highly likely to have been the same gun that killed them both. I think it was Giles who brought that up. But Marcus and I had the photographs in common and if I'd come forward saying that Bobby, or Tom, was my brother, you know what the prosecution might have made of that - I was having an affair with Marcus and my brother objected. Marcus was on his way to kill him but someone got there first."

"As I understand matters, the police have no additional evidence and I doubt now they're going to find any. A personal friend of mine within the forensic pathology team told me that Harry Henry was given a truth drug; scopolamine, mixed with an ethanol based substance. No one is speculating on why that was but the theory is that both murders were done by a professional. Henry had many enemies, as did your brother, Alicia, albeit not as numerous. Marcus had no option but to admit he was carrying a gun. I couldn't see how it helped raising disagreements or clashes of temperament there may have been between Rupert and Alicia's brother, or Alicia knowing Marcus Allenby. Personally I think the three years he was sentenced to for carrying an offensive weapon was lenient, whereas carrying a weapon with intent to kill carries a life sentence as punishment." Giles stared directly at Rupert, refuting his allegation of underachieving at the trial. "He'll be out in two, if not sooner." Rupert did not comment on Giles's remarks, but he did have something to say to my sister.

"I've just been wondering if you killed him to stop him claiming any part of the hugely wealthy estate Mary must have left you. Yes, that news found a way onto the streets and it wasn't carried by *The Courier* either. I wonder if that's the real reason why you never stepped up?" Rupert's eyes narrowed in his unmistaken suspicion.

"Firstly he couldn't have any claim on her and secondly, where do you think Alicia got a gun, Rupert? Besides, she was me," Giles leapt to Alice's defence.

The table was being cleared as Alice, with Giles sitting beside her, finished the evening with glasses of brandy and port alongside an assortment of after-dinner bites in the lounge next to the room where the meal was served. Rupert and Susan sat the opposite side of the oblong glass coffee table. Rupert had more to say.

"The police interviewed both Marcus and me over a letter found in your brother's apartment in Mayfair commenting on the cost of funerals. Did they ask you about it, Alicia?"

"They did and you know why they did. You told them I was at your home to take your photograph when Marcus was there. They were satisfied that I had nothing to do with a letter."

"I still don't know why you didn't say he was your brother." This time it was Susan.

"Exactly," Rupert had found an ally. "When the police were questioning you about that letter why didn't you pipe up then?"

"I thought I explained that. I have no real idea how the minds of policemen work, but I thought it would have confused the issue, that's all." My sister's disconsolate gaze fell on Giles, who smiled back trying to reassure her.

"It was my advice," Giles declared as he refilled Rupert's and his own glass, offering Susan and Alicia, who both refused. "There was nothing I could do for Marcus more than I did, so why rock the boat by giving the police someone else to dig away at!"

"Civic duty?" Susan offered, with a frown biting into her forehead and eyes as wide as the window she sat in front of.

"Was that what you called the headlines and editorials in *The Courier* you wrote some time ago about a sex scandal, Susan? Because it wouldn't be what I would call it." Giles jumped in.

"What my ex and that puritanical Tomlinson were doing was not only morally wrong, it was illegal, Giles. It didn't take a QC to fathom that sorry story out. He was paying local government officials to get children to have sex with. I was exposing a scandal of vital importance to this country." She fell silent as if in deep thought.

"One thing I don't understand, Giles." It was Alice this time with a question. "Is why didn't Marcus dump his gun in the Thames after seeing Bobby Brown was already dead? He wouldn't have been charged with anything had he done that."

"I asked him the same question. Said it must have been shock. That's when we used it to his advantage in the only way I saw possible. The fear of running through the park at that time of night necessitated the carrying of that weapon. Yes, okay, it's admitting to carrying a weapon, but what else could we do? At least it was some mitigation."

"What was the reason he gave for carrying a gun?" Alice asked.

"I never asked him that."

"Would that be to avoid the possibility of hearing the truth and having to tell the jury, Giles?" It was Susan who directed the question of truth at the Queen's Counsel.

"I saw no advantage in asking the question, Susan. What on earth could the man say other than something to incriminate himself? I wanted to deal with what we had rather the conjecture surrounding a dead body with a man and a gun close by."

"You have a valid objection, my learned friend," with a smile Susan replied.

"You're very quiet, Rupert. Got anything you want to add?" Giles asked.

"Not really, other than I do see Alicia's point of staying out of it all. With the police questioning the girl that Brown brought to my club in Manchester, it couldn't have helped Marcus who saw her quite regularly. If Alicia stuck her hand up and said, 'Excuse me but that was my brother in the park' it could have stirred things up. I go along with her and you, Giles. I can see how it all could have gone topsy-turvy."

"Who owns the Kiss Club now? Do you know, Giles?" Alice asked.

"I can answer that. I do, Alicia," it was Rupert who replied. "The agreement I had with Henry is still in place. Tomlinson set up a company to buy him out when he lost a pot of money following Marcus's investment recommendations. That was another reason why the police looked so closely at Marcus with the Tomlinson suicide."

"And you said earlier that I'd let you down over that, Rupert, where in actual fact it was my foresight that pulled it off." Giles jumped in again looking for an apology.

"By default, then yes, Giles, I owe you that." The two touched glasses as Susan poured another glass of port and Alice joined her.

"Did you kill Henry, Rupert?"

"No, Susan, I did not. Did you?" he countered.

"Do you know that the only one here who we haven't asked is you, Giles? How do you plead?" my sister asked.

"To which charge or to them both?" he replied with a wide smile.

"Let's try the murder of Alicia's brother. After all, you live the closest to where he was shot and you certainly would not want a brother-in-law like him. No offence, Alicia," Rupert's smug smile had returned.

"I was, as I said, home here asleep with Alicia by my side at the time he died. So I'm pleased to say that we both have alibis. The only one who had a dubious alibi was Marcus, but as I just said we worked on that and arrived at where we did."

"Which leaves us searching for a murderer," Alice added in between satisfying sips from her glass.

"That's if you want to look, Alicia. I for one won't be joining the search party," Susan made her position perfectly clear.

Part Eighteen

"Let's analyse what we've got and make a decision. Feel free to throw anything you want into the pile as we go. Okay?" Detective Chief Inspector George Warner was holding yet another briefing session on the first floor CID auxiliary offices at Battersea Police Station. His team of seven detectives looked bored, overworked and tired.

"It's been three weeks since the discovery of our two victims:—" he turned to a 'situation-board' and pointed at two photographs "—Photo A: Mr Harry Henry, the proprietor of the Kiss Club, and photo B: Bobby Brown, also known as Tom Collins, who worked for our first victim. Let's list what we got: Two spent bullets. One from the floor in the flat above the Kiss Club that had exited from the head of victim A, and one from a tree in Battersea Park where victim B was found. Both were 9 mm shells, but no cartridge cases were discovered. Both victims were shot at close range. An execution job carried out professionally. No witnesses, nobody out walking their dog in Battersea Park or canoeing along the Thames around two in the morning.

"Nobody hearing a single gunshot, or any unusual noise from the flat above the Kiss Club, in Dean Street, around midnight. We have a discarded hypodermic syringe found in a dustbin in Richmond Buildings, at the rear of the Kiss Club, which has traces of the drug that was found in victim A. Apparently this caused his heart to stop before he was shot. Quite frankly, boys and girls, we have bugger all."

"I've got some overtime due on my card though, guv," shouted an optimistic detective constable. DCI Warner chose to smile at the remark, but not comment on it.

"Times being what they are, and finances always being a consideration—" he glanced towards where the interruption had come from "—should we spend more time on this case involving two known criminals that we no longer have to bother with, or do we cut our losses and archive the files?"

After a short discussion where the shared opinion was unanimous in deciding there was nothing to gain from continuing the investigation, DCI Warner thanked his assembled team and dismissed them back to divisional duties. As desks and workstations were being emptied and a noise akin to children breaking up for a school holiday began to grow in decibels, Warner caught the eye of his sergeant, who beckoned him to her office in the adjoining room.

"I thought you were going to stay on this case for a couple more days, guv. I know the Special Branch involvement got up your nose and like you, I'd have thought they would have allowed access to the report on the spent shells by now, but you must still be thinking we're looking for an IRA gunman. Nothing has changed there, has it?"

"I don't think we will ever get to see the forensic report on those bullets, Sarah. Nor do I think they went to Special Branch. I think they went straight to the Home Office in Whitehall.

"What makes you think that, guv?"

"I had the person who signed the receipt book at forensics traced. Drew a dead end. File said, quote: Restricted to HMG Access. She's a spook with the intelligence service or my name is Harry Henry."

* * *

One either acquires the quality of being honest along the path of life or one does not. To become an accomplished liar or thief takes time, and to succeed in either requires astute practice or the liar is found out and the thief is quickly apprehended. But honesty is not just about resisting that tempting unguarded wallet open and staring at you from the counter of a shop. It can become a manner of living whereby every thought and action is governed by truth and sincerity. Sir Giles Milton had a point in saying the truth is not always unambiguous and justice is not dependent on truth.

Honesty manifests itself in many forms; one being the withholding of secrets, or information a person tells you in confidence. The disclosure of such a secret for your own benefit is perfidious as well as being disloyal. Alice knew Paula had not been loyal towards some elements involved in the so-called Troubles of Ireland, but that was hardly her affair. In an honest, principled world my sister would not have repeated Paula's confession to a living soul, let alone who she did. Then again in a virtuous world there would be no need for Alice to pay for an Irish murderer, the one respectful Paula recommended to shoot me. As far as I know contract killers are loyal to only one thing and that's not politics or religious beliefs; it is money, something Alice wasn't short of. Harry Henry was pumped full of scopolamine in order to find out where I was that night and then shot in the head to spread the blame for my murder as far away from Alice as was humanly possible. You see, when Paula accepted my sister on face value she made a costly mistake, but an even bigger one was telling an Irish murderer that there was a need for his skills on the mainland of Britain where he would met his paymaster.

No one will link the gentle passing of an elderly lady whilst she slept in Valley End, near Galway, far removed from the frontline Secret Services of the United Kingdom, with that of two criminals in London and neither Giles, Susan, Rupert nor Marcus had ever heard of Paula Fitzgerald; God rest her soul.

Dear reader,

We hope you enjoyed reading *The Story That Had No Beginning*. Please take a moment to leave a review, even if it's a short one. Your opinion is important to us.

Discover more books by Daniel Kemp at https://www.nextchapter.pub/authors/daniel-kemp-mystery-thriller-author

Want to know when one of our books is free or discounted? Join the newsletter at http://eepurl.com/bqqB3H

Best regards,
Daniel Kemp and the Next Chapter Team

About the Author

Danny Kemp, ex-London police officer, mini-cab business owner, pub tenant and licensed London taxi driver, never planned to be a writer, but after his first novel —The Desolate Garden — was under a paid option to become a $30 million film for five years until distribution became an insurmountable problem for the production company what else could he do?

Nowadays he is a prolific storyteller, and although it's true to say that he mainly concentrates on what he knows most about; murders laced by the intrigue involving spies, his diverse experience of life shows in the short stories he compiles both for adults and children.

He is the recipient of rave reviews from a prestigious Manhattan publication, been described as —the new Graham Green — by a managerial employee of Waterstones Books, for whom he did a countrywide tour of signing events, and he has appeared on 'live' nationwide television.

http://www-thedesolategarden-com.co.uk/

The Story That Had No Beginning
ISBN: 978-4-86752-633-0 (Mass Market)

Published by
Next Chapter
1-60-20 Minami-Otsuka
170-0005 Toshima-Ku, Tokyo
+818035793528
4th August 2021

www.ingramcontent.com/pod-product-compliance
Lightning Source LLC
LaVergne TN
LVHW032009070526
838202LV00059B/6361